the fall of candy corn

To my parents, Rick and Barbara Reynolds, who love Disneyland and all theme parks and passed that love along to me.
I would like to thank everyone who has helped me through the course of writing this book. Thank you to my husband, Scott, and to all my friends who listened as I described the theme park in detail. Thank you to my agent, Beth Jusino, for believing in me. Thank you to Barbara Scott and the group at Zonderkidz who championed the story. Thank you all.

A Sweet Seasons Novel

the fall of candy corn

debbie viguié

ZONDERVAN.com/
AUTHORTRACKER
follow your favorite authors

ZONDERVAN®

The Fall of Candy Corn
Copyright © 2008 by Debbie Viguié

Requests for information should be addressed to:

Zondervan, *Grand Rapids, Michigan 49530*

Library of Congress Cataloging-in-Publication Data: Applied for

ISBN 978-0-310-71559-7

Published in association with the literary agency of Alive Communications, Inc., 7680 Goddard Street, Suite 200, Colorado Springs, Colorado 80920. www.alivecommunications.com

Interior design by Christine Orejuela-Winkelman

Printed in the United States of America

08 09 10 11 12 13 14 • 23 22 21 20 19 18 17 16 15 14 13 12 11 10 9 8 7 6 5 4 3 2 1

the fall of candy corn

1

Candace Thompson knew she was crazy. That was the only possible explanation for why, once again, she was sitting across the desk from Lloyd Peterson, hiring manager for The Zone theme park. A lot had changed since the day in June when she had been hired to operate a cotton candy machine. Still, sitting across from Lloyd, she felt self-conscious and a bit insecure.

"So," he said, staring at her intently. "You think you can be a maze monster for Scare?"

She nodded. Scare was what they called the annual Halloween event at The Zone. Aside from putting frightening elements in traditional rides, during Scare there were a dozen mazes where monsters did their best to scare park guests as they wound their way through dark and creepy corridors.

"Then show me something scary."

It was eleven in the morning in a brightly lit office. What on earth did he expect of her? She wanted to say something smart. She wanted to say something funny. With horror she realized she didn't have *anything* to say.

"Come on, come on," he said. "Be a monster, jump around, growl, something."

She got out of her seat and did the best growl she could. Unfortunately, she sounded less like a monster and more like a frightened Chihuahua.

"Threaten me!"

She got closer to him than she would have liked, jumped up and down, swung her arms, and pounded her fist firmly on his desk. She could tell by the look on his face that he wasn't impressed.

She growled again and yelled, "I'm going to get you!" She felt like the world's biggest idiot. No one would be scared of a teenage girl, especially not one wearing a gray business suit and sensible shoes.

"Scream!" he ordered.

She threw back her head and screamed her loudest, shrill-est scream. That, at least, was easy. It was a game her best friend, Tamara, and she had played when they were little. They had competitions to see who could scream louder or longer or higher.

She screamed for ten seconds and then sat back down in her chair. She expected Lloyd to laugh; she expected him to say something derisive. Instead, he looked at her thoughtfully.

"I have the perfect role for you to play," he said. He wrote something on an orange slip of paper. "You're going to be Candy in the Candy Craze maze."

"Candy?" she asked questioningly. "Am I going to be dressed up like a giant Twix bar or something?"

He shook his head. "Nothing like that. You should be proud; it's our latest maze. The lines for it will wrap halfway through the park."

He handed her a stack of papers. "You can go fill these out. Then Saturday at nine a.m. report to the costume warehouse for your fitting and orientation. At that time you'll also be able to pick up your badge, ID, and parking pass."

"Saturday at nine," she confirmed as she took the stack from him.

"There's a table—"

"Out in the courtyard," she finished for him.

Since she was a returning referee—which was the The Zone's name for an employee—there was slightly less paperwork this time. There was, however, an entire book of rules and policies regarding Scare. She had to sign several forms stating that she had received it, she had read it, she had understood it, and she promised to abide by it. It seemed like the golden rule of Scare was *"thou shalt have no physical contact of any kind with players." Players* was what they called the customers. Touching a player during Scare apparently was grounds for immediate dismissal.

Once she finished filling out and signing all her paperwork, she returned it to Lloyd Peterson.

Checking her watch, she discovered that she still had an hour before she had to meet Tamara for a late lunch. She decided to head into the theme park to see a few friends.

The first thing she noticed when she entered the park was that the Holiday Zone was closed. Temporary walls set up around the area prevented players from going inside or even getting a peek at what was going on.

The Holiday Zone was one of nine themed areas inside The Zone theme park. The theme of the Holiday Zone changed throughout the year to reflect different holidays. It was the day after Labor Day so all the Fourth of July themes from summer were now being replaced with Halloween themes for fall. The transformation would take about ten days, and then the Holiday Zone would be open again for business.

Several key attractions throughout the rest of the park were also closed, getting their Scare overlay. The Muffin Mansion was one of them, she discovered when she went there looking for her friend Becca. The Muffin Mansion was unique in the park because half of it was in the Exploration Zone and half of it was in the History Zone. The Exploration Zone half was located near most of the kitchens, which looked a lot more like laboratories.

There was a small counter where they sold the muffins. The side that was in the History Zone looked like an old-fashioned mansion, and guests could eat their muffins at one of the tables scattered around the parlor. It was from the History side that it got its name. It was from the Exploration side that it got its wild concoctions of muffins and its ever-expanding menu.

She stared for a moment at the construction walls around the building and wondered what the Muffin Mansion would look like when the walls came down. She also wondered where Becca was working while the mansion was getting its Halloween makeover. She glanced at her watch and thought about who else she might be able to track down to chat with.

She knew that two of her other friends, Josh and Roger, had ended their summer jobs and weren't there. Fortunately, both of them were going to be working Scare. They had managed to talk her into joining them. Spending time with them was one of the best perks of working the event. One of the others was that it paid slightly more than her summer job had.

Martha, her former supervisor, spent a lot of time off field in the employee-only areas. Candace wasn't sure if Sue, one of her other friends, had already quit her summer job as a janitor or not. That left Kurt. So Candace made her way to the History Zone.

Kurt was her boyfriend. The word was still exciting and new to Candace. He worked as a mascot, a costumed character. They had met the day she first became a Zone referee and, after some rocky moments, had ended the summer as a couple. She found him dressed like Robin Hood in the medieval area of the History Zone. She had gotten good at recognizing his dark hair and brilliant blue eyes no matter what costume or mask he was wearing.

"Hey, gorgeous!" he said, when he saw her, and he gave her a quick kiss.

"Eeeww!" a little boy holding an autograph book said.

"She's not Maid Marion," the boy's sister protested.

"She's not?" Kurt asked, feigning surprise.

"I don't think Maid Marion has red hair," another little girl commented.

Kurt turned back to Candace, "Away lady, for you are not my dearest love."

Candace pretended to be crushed and put her hand to her forehead as though she might faint. The children laughed at that. "But I am! I am wearing this disguise to hide from the evil Prince John."

"Robin will protect you!" the little girl said excitedly.

The little boy handed Candace his autograph book with great solemnity. She signed Maid Marion's name, and he seemed immensely pleased.

After the children left, Kurt smiled at her. "Nice job."

"Thank you. I'm practicing my acting skills for Scare."

"You signed up?"

"Just now."

"That's great! What did you get?"

"Apparently it's the new maze. I'm playing Candy."

Kurt looked startled, but before he could say anything, he was besieged by several more children wanting pictures and autographs. Soon a line formed. Candace glanced at her watch, and Kurt shrugged and gave her a smile. She waved good-bye and headed for the front of the park.

Twenty minutes later she was sitting with Tamara in their favorite ice cream parlor.

"Want to split the turkey sandwich and a banana split?" Tamara asked.

"Split the split? You took the words right out of my mouth," Candace said.

After the waitress took their order, they discussed the fact that they had only a few hours of freedom left before school started up in the morning.

"I can't believe we only have two classes together this year," Tamara complained.

"At least one of them is homeroom," Candace said.

"Drama should be fun though," Tamara said.

"I can't believe I let you talk me into signing up for that."

"Come on, you're going to be a maze monster. What's a little acting to you?" Tamara teased.

Candace smiled. "I am pretty jazzed about that," she admitted. "I just hope I do a good job. I totally couldn't pull off 'scary' in front of the recruiter today. I should thank you, though. I got a position based on my ability to scream."

"You're welcome," Tamara said. "See, all those hours in the garage paid off."

"You're going to come see me in the maze, right?"

Tamara was adventurous, but she hated anything that resembled a monster or something that went bump in the night. She couldn't stand horror films and hadn't even been able to make it through the old movie *Jaws* the year before without freaking out and vowing never to go swimming in the ocean again.

"I guess if you're going to overcome your fear of mazes enough to work in one, the least I can do is come see you in it," Tamara said with a heavy sigh.

"You're the best."

"I know."

After lunch they did some last-minute school shopping, and each of them ended up with pencils, paper, and three pairs of shoes.

"Seriously, I don't think I can wear these to school," Candace said, pulling a pair of three-inch black heels out of one of the bags.

"Then you can wear them *after* school when you go out with Kurt," Tamara said. "That officially makes them 'school adjacent' and so, school shoes."

"You have messed-up logic, Tam, but I love it."

"Knew you would."

They headed back to Candace's house so she could change clothes before youth group. While Tamara unpacked her shoes for her, Candace threw on a pair of jeans and a Zone sweatshirt she had borrowed from Kurt.

"You're never giving him back that sweatshirt, are you?" Tamara said.

"Not if I can help it," Candace laughed. "Besides, it's the duty of a girlfriend to swipe some article of clothing from her boyfriend. It's like a sacred trust. The guy carries around a picture of the girl, and the girl snags his sweatshirt."

"You weren't even cold the other night at the theater when you got that, were you?"

"I'll never tell," Candace said with a laugh.

When they left the house and headed for church, Candace was both excited and a little nervous. Because of her summer job, she had missed out on youth group all summer. Now she was returning and she was officially a senior. It would be her first senior-y thing.

Once they arrived and entered the familiar building, though, she began to relax. The youth building was large and furnished with old beat-up couches, chairs, and plenty of pillows for sprawling on the floor. Almost a hundred people were in attendance. The freshmen were easy to spot with their wide-eyed looks of excitement. They had finally entered the major leagues, and it was a big night for them too.

Candace and Tamara staked their claim to one of the smaller couches just before the youth pastor, Bobby, called everyone together. They prayed and then sang a couple of praise songs.

"Okay, welcome, everyone, to a new year. We're glad to see all you freshers out there. And seniors, congratulations on being the top dogs."

There was a weak yell from the freshmen, which was dwarfed by the shout of the seniors. The sophomores looked relieved that they were no longer freshmen, while the juniors looked enviously at the seniors.

"Make sure you take a fall schedule home tonight. We've got a lot of great events coming up in the next couple of months.

There's the girls' all-night party next Friday night. Don't forget the annual all-church marathon the following Sunday. We'll have a guest band at the end of the month, which I know you won't want to miss. We're also doing something brand new this year. The first Friday in October we'll get on buses and head on over to Scare at The Zone!"

Cheers went up from almost everyone in the room. Candace was stunned. She knew a lot of church youth groups went to Scare, but this was the first year her youth group was planning on it. She began to rethink her employment options. It was going to be weird enough playing a monster on display in a maze without her entire youth group there to see her. Slowly, she sank down lower on the couch, willing herself to be unseen.

Tamara waved her hand in the air, and, before Candace could stop her, Bobby called, "What is it Tamara?"

"I just thought everyone would like to know that Candace is going to be a monster in one of the mazes."

Candace could feel her cheeks burning as she glared at Tamara.

"Hear that everyone? Make sure you come with us to Scare, and you can see Candace at work!"

There were more cheers as Candace sat there in dismay.

A freshman girl raised her hand.

"Yes, what's your name?" Bobby asked.

"Jen. How much will Scare cost?" she asked, clearly concerned.

"Well, Jen, that's the best part. This is the perfect time to invite out all your friends—Christians and non-Christians. The entire event, including entrance ticket, transportation, food, and a souvenir T-shirt, is completely sponsored. So it's free!"

And now, with the exception of Candace, there was a standing ovation. Candace just glared up at Tamara. "This is your fault, isn't it?" she asked.

Tamara just smiled innocently. "I have to support my best friend, don't I?"

Candace thought that maybe she could use a little less support and a lot more privacy, but she didn't say so. Tamara's entire family was beyond rich. Tamara and Candace had been friends before either of them even understood what was up with money. Most of the time Tamara played it casual, but every once in a while she did something generous and outrageous. This time her generosity was going to put Candace fully in the spotlight. As cool as it often was to have a friend with money, there was a downside.

"How could you do that to me?" Candace asked when she and Tamara were back in the car after youth group was over.

"I love you, Cand, but if you think I'm going through those mazes by myself, you're crazy. I plan on putting as many bodies between me and the guys in the scary masks as possible."

"But I'm one of the guys in the scary masks! Besides, it's perfectly safe. They're not allowed to touch players at all."

"That's what you say."

"It's true. It says so in the handbook."

Tamara rolled her eyes. "Sure, and how many people aside from you bothered to read it?"

"That's not fair. It's in the pamphlet too," Candace protested.

"Oh, and because it says so in the pamphlet it must be true," Tamara said. "Maybe if they posted it on the Web it would be doubly true."

"Knock it off," Candace said, still irritated and in no mood to play.

"Seriously, you're not worried are you?" Tamara asked, doing her best to stop smiling.

"No, I love being in the spotlight," Candace said, letting the sarcasm flow freely. "Hello! Remember me? Your best friend? I hang around with you so I can be spotlight adjacent, as in, not *in* but nearby."

"Well you need the drama class worse than I thought," Tamara said.

"I don't want to be in the spotlight."

Tamara pulled up in front of Candace's house and parked. "You know," she said, her voice suddenly very thoughtful, "for someone who doesn't want to be in the spotlight, you seem to spend a lot of time in it lately."

"Hello? Not my fault," Candace said.

"I'm not saying it is," Tamara answered, putting her hand on Candace's shoulder. "I just think you seem to end up there no matter what you do. I mean you were a cotton candy operator all summer, and how many times did you name something at the park or win some competition or otherwise draw everyone's attention your way?"

"Too many," Candace muttered.

"Exactly. Stuff like that doesn't just happen. I think maybe God's trying to tell you something."

"Like what?"

"Like maybe you're not meant to live your life spotlight adjacent. Maybe you're meant to be front and center."

Candace was quiet for a moment while she thought about that. It seemed like such a crazy idea. She had always lived in a way that ensured she blended into the background. The thought of standing apart from it was intimidating. Yet, hadn't she done exactly that when she and her team won The Zone Scavenger Hunt? Or the time she stood up for her rights when she was falsely accused at work? That hadn't exactly been blending in.

She shook her head. It was a lot to think about, and the part of her brain that was already freaked out *so* didn't want to go there. "Maybe it's just coincidence," she said.

"I don't believe in coincidence," Tamara said. "I believe in plans God makes and doesn't tell you about until later."

Candace smiled. "Any chance God plans to make it snow or something so we don't have to go to school tomorrow?"

Tamara looked at the readout on her dashboard. "It's nine thirty at night, and it's still eighty-seven degrees outside. Besides, this is Southern California. When God makes it snow here, it's not a plan; it's a miracle."

Candace couldn't help but laugh at that. "Thanks, Tam," she said after a minute.

"Hey, that's what friends are for," she said with a shrug. "Wanna carpool tomorrow?"

Candace nodded. "You driving or me?"

"I will. See you in the morning."

Once in her room Candace thought about calling Kurt or her friend Josh. Reason won out, though, since she had school in the morning, and calling either of them could result in her being up way too late.

"Morning's going to come awfully early," she confided in Mr. Huggles, her stuffed bear.

2

As it was, the morning came earlier than expected. Candace was having a nightmare about showing up to school naked when she heard the sound of rushing water and then woke up when she registered her dad's voice shouting in alarm.

She sat up straight in bed, and the water sound didn't go away. She saw her mother fly by her door on the way to the stairs. Candace jumped out of bed and went to the top of the stairs.

"What's wrong?" she shouted down.

"Pipe broke," her father shouted back.

As she rubbed the sleep from her eyes, Candace began to see exactly what was wrong. There was standing water in the living room. Within a minute, the sound of rushing water faded as her dad turned off the water to the house.

Candace moved carefully down the stairs and finally took a seat halfway down. From there she could see it wasn't just the living room. There was water everywhere downstairs.

Her parents regrouped at the bottom of the stairs, causing ripples in the water. They looked pretty upset.

Under the circumstances, asking them if everything was okay seemed like the wrong thing. "What happened?"

"Pipe broke in the bathroom," her dad said. "I heard water running, and I thought you must be awake. It didn't turn off, though, so I got up and found this," he said, indicating the water around him.

"I'm sorry," Candace said.

"It's not your fault, honey," her dad said.

"I know. I just feel bad that it happened."

"It will be okay," her mom said tiredly. "We were thinking it was time to replace the carpet anyway."

"Plus we've got insurance," her dad said.

"So everything is going to be okay?" Candace asked.

"Well, not for several days, but it will all turn out," her mom said, moving to join her on the stairs. "At least this didn't happen upstairs. Then we'd have two floors to worry about, not to mention water damage to the ceiling."

She reached out and patted Candace on the knee.

"We should all pack some clothes and whatever else we'll need for a couple of days," her dad said. "We're going to have plumbers and carpenters traipsing through here, ripping things out and setting up huge fans to dry everything out that they can. We'll have to stay in a hotel for a couple of days."

"I know it's terrible timing with school starting today. You could stay with Tamara if you like," her mom suggested.

Candace leaned down and gave her mom a quick hug. "Thanks."

"We should all go upstairs and get what we'll need," her dad said, starting up the stairs.

Candace stood up and made her way back to her room where she tried to decide what to pack.

🍁

Three hours later Tamara pulled up outside. Her eyes widened as Candace sloshed out of the front door with her snow boots on and several duffel bags slung over her shoulders.

"You know it isn't a snow day, right?" Tamara called.

Candace waved behind her to where water was still seeping out onto the porch. Tamara popped the trunk for Candace, and she stowed her backpack and other bags inside. Candace took off the snow boots and slipped on her school shoes. She then ran the snow boots back up to the front door and set them beside the porch.

Once she got into the car she heaved a sigh.

"Wow! Your parents finally took that whole sink-or-swim thing literally?" Tamara asked.

"Pipe broke," Candace said. "It happened in the middle of the night. The first floor's flooded."

"You can't stay here while they're fixing it."

Candace shook her head.

"You wanna stay with me?" Tamara asked, eyes widening even more in excitement.

"I thought you'd never ask," Candace said, forcing a smile.

"As if. This rocks! We are going to have so much fun," Tamara said.

Candace relaxed into the seat. Tamara was right. It was an awesome way to kick off senior year.

Twenty minutes later they parked in the student parking lot. They sat for a moment in silence and stared at the cars and people streaming by. Some faces were familiar to Candace, while others were not. One of her classmates parked nearby. He got out with his kid sister, who was just starting high school, in tow. Neither of them looked happy to be sharing the same school, let alone the same car.

Tamara pointed to a group of freshman girls clustered together at the end of one of the buildings, obviously building up their courage. "Remember when that was us?"

"Please, that was never *us*. That was me, cowering in your shadow. Even back then you were completely sure of yourself. Course, it didn't hurt that you were already dating that junior ... what was his name?"

"Stan. Or as I like to call him, Stank. What a creep!"

Candace laughed. "On that note, I think it's time we go forth and conquer."

It was weird stepping foot on campus and knowing that she was a senior—top of the food chain. It was even stranger still to think that in a year she would be stepping onto a new campus where once again she would be at the bottom of the food chain. She took a deep breath and resolved that no matter how much planning she had to do for the next year, she wouldn't let it stop her from enjoying the current one.

"Hi, Tamara."

"Hi, Tamara."

Two girls stopped in front of them, blocking their path. One was brunette and the other blonde with Barbie-like appearances right down to the slightly plastic look of their smiles.

Candace scowled. Amanda and Kristen were snobs. They always had been. Candace knew Tamara had hung out with them some over the summer when she and Tamara were fighting. Nothing seemed to have changed. Both girls were eager to talk to Tamara but purposely ignored Candace. Any other year she would have just stood there and taken it. But it was senior year, and she wasn't the same Candace she had been before the summer.

"Ladies, we're in a hurry, so unless you have something meaningful to say to either me or my friend, kindly get out of our way."

"What?" Kristen asked, momentarily thrown.

"You heard me. Come on, Tam," Candace said, shouldering Amanda aside.

Tamara followed her, and, after they had left the Barbie twins behind, she started laughing. "Candace, I like the whole assertive thing. Did you see the look on Kristen's face? I thought she was going to hurt her brain."

"I'm tired of being ignored," Candace said.

"Good. Of course, that just puts you one step closer to the spotlight," Tamara said.

"You are not even allowed to gloat," Candace said.

"Come on! Not even a little?"

"Not even a tiny bit."

Tamara sighed in exaggerated frustration.

The morning flew by, and her last class before lunch quickly arrived. Unfortunately, with Mr. Tuttle for history, her fast-paced day came to a screeching halt. She had to struggle to keep herself awake.

The man spoke in a monotone and read from his notes, never looking up. He also had the most irritating way of taking some interesting area of history and picking the most obscure, boring details to talk about. As a result, half the class was asleep by the time the bell rang for lunch.

Candace dragged herself to her feet, trying to shake off the malaise that had taken hold. Once outside the class, she flipped open her phone and saw that she had just missed a call from Kurt. She called him back, and he answered on the first ring.

"I was hoping you'd call," he said.

"Lunch just started," she said. "What's up?"

"I wanted to see how your first day back was going."

"Nothing I can't handle so far," she said. "So, you never told me, what are you doing for Scare?"

"I'm working as an umpire in the Horrific History maze."

Candace wrinkled her nose. "Is it based on Mr. Tuttle's class? Because he can take any subject and make it horrifically boring." She suddenly turned around, hoping that Mr. Tuttle hadn't magically appeared behind her. She was safe. The teacher was nowhere in sight.

Kurt laughed, and the sound made Candace feel warm inside. "Not quite. Think Lizzie Borden, Jack the Ripper, and Nero laughing and playing the fiddle while Rome burned."

"You win, that is definitely more horrific than one of his lectures," Candace admitted, shivering slightly just thinking about it. Maybe working Scare was a bad idea. She had never even attended one before. She was terrified of mazes, and, since Tamara hated to be scared, there had never been an impetus to go before. What on earth had she been thinking? For a moment she thought of calling it off. No one would blame her. She could say that she realized she just couldn't juggle school and work. Tamara would know the truth, though, and she'd never let her forget it, especially since she was paying for everyone in youth group to come.

"Candace, you there?"

Candace blushed as she realized she had just missed whatever Kurt had been saying. "Yes, I'm here. So, what's an umpire? I'm guessing it's not the baseball guy."

Kurt laughed again. "Umpires are the ones who wear all black and are in the mazes to help people and keep an eye on the characters. Think of us as maze security meets guest services."

"Why are you going to be an umpire? You're a mascot. Isn't this like the best time of year for you?"

He laughed. "It's a tradition that all mascots work as umpires for Scare. Since we wear costumes every other day that we work here, they lose some of their magic."

"Ah, so wearing black clothes and standing in the background is like your costume."

"Exactly."

"That's cool." She thought about asking him just how scary the mazes were but was too embarrassed. She didn't want her boyfriend to think she was a total wimp.

"Well, break's over. I gotta go," he said.

"Okay, talk to you later," she said.

"Bye."

She stared at the phone for a minute. There was one person she could ask about Scare—one person she could trust not to laugh. She decided to call Josh after school.

After school they drove straight to Tamara's house. They unloaded Candace's bags and took them upstairs to the guest room next to Tamara's room. Despite Candace's protests, the maid set about unpacking her things.

"There's no reasoning with her once her mind is set," Tamara advised. "Best to just let her."

"Miss Tamara, your parents are going to be late tonight. They said you and Miss Candace could do what you liked."

"Thanks," Tamara said.

Candace grabbed a pair of jeans and a tank top from her bag before the maid could transfer them to the closet, and she slipped into her private bathroom to change. Remembering that she wanted to give Josh a call, she slipped her cell into her pocket. A minute later she rejoined Tamara in the hall. Her friend had also changed, and they headed downstairs.

"Movies and pizza work for you?" Tamara asked.

"Don't they always?" Candace asked.

Her phone rang, and she nearly tripped on the last stair in surprise.

"Your pants are ringing," Tamara said, smirking.

Candace pulled the phone out. "It's Josh," she said before answering. "Hey! I was thinking of calling you."

"Great minds think alike," Josh said. "What's going on?"

"Pipes broke at home in the middle of the night. I'm staying with Tamara for a few days."

"Bummer about the pipes. I'm sure you'll have a lot of fun though."

"You know it," Candace laughed. "The last time Tam and I got to have a sleepover on a school night was in fourth grade when her mom had surgery."

Suddenly, Tamara snatched the phone from Candace's hand. Candace stared at her startled. "What?"

Tamara smiled impishly and spoke into the phone. "I'm sorry, I'm officially holding Cand's phone hostage."

Candace tried to take her phone back, but Tamara kept dodging around furniture in the living room.

"No. Yes."

"What's going on?" Candace asked.

"Uh-huh. She is."

"Give me the phone."

"Pizza and movies. Wanna join us?"

"What?" Candace asked.

"1512 Willow Way. Yeah. Brick outside—you can't miss it. See you."

Tamara hung up and tossed the phone back to Candace. "He's coming over."

"What did you do that for?" Candace asked.

"Because he's cool, and I thought it would be fun."

Candace still hadn't gotten over how jealous Tamara had been of Josh and her other friends from The Zone for most of the summer. It just seemed weird that she was so willing to hang out with him after all that. A sudden thought occurred to her. "You like him, don't you?"

"Yeah, he's cool," Tamara said, giving her a where-have-you-been look.

"No, I mean *like him* like him."

Tamara stopped for a moment as if the thought was completely new to her. "He's cute and funny," Tamara said musingly. "But, I don't think I like him in that way."

"Why not?" Candace asked, warming to the thought of two of her best friends getting together.

"I don't know. It's just not ... right. I don't know how else to explain it."

Candace decided not to push, though the more she thought about it the more she liked the idea.

"So, double pepperoni?" Tamara asked, changing the subject.

"Is there any other kind?" Candace laughed.

"I've heard rumors, but I haven't been able to verify," Tamara said.

She ordered the pizza, and they both sat down on the couch. "Who do you think will get here first, Josh or the pizza guy?" Tamara asked.

"I've got dibs on the pizza guy," Candace said.

"Candace, you're dating someone. I don't think you can claim dibs on the pizza guy," Tamara said seriously.

Candace threw a pillow at her. "Not what I meant."

Tamara threw the pillow back. "Just checking."

As it turned out, they arrived at the same time. The doorbell rang, and when Tamara and Candace went to answer it, they found Josh on the step paying the pizza delivery guy. Josh was tall with sandy hair and a great smile. Candace and Josh had become friends over the summer, bonding over sharing their secrets with each other. Josh had never told anyone how Candace felt about Kurt, and she, in turn, had never breathed a word of his secret to anyone.

Josh took the pizza and stepped inside. "Did someone call for pizza?" he joked.

"Let me pay for that," Tamara said, fishing money out of her pocket.

"It's okay, I've got it. Mom said never to show up to a party empty-handed, and this way I haven't."

"Please. You can't get paid that much from The Zone," Tamara said.

Candace bit her lip. She elbowed Tamara.

"Ow! What?"

"What has your mom said about gentlemen?"

Tamara wrinkled her nose. "Always let them pay when they offer and never feel obligated because of that."

"So?"

Tamara sighed and rolled her eyes. "Fine. Thank you for the pizza, Joshua, but you're not getting a kiss for it."

Josh stared at her like she had grown a second head. "Uh …
not looking for one."

"Good!" Tamara said, grabbing the pizza and leading the
way back to the living room.

Josh looked at Candace. She just shrugged, and he shook
his head. They then joined Tamara in the living room.

3

A large pizza and two movies later, Candace, Josh, and Tamara were laughing so hard they were crying. Tamara had just finished telling Josh about how the entire youth group was coming to the Scare and how Candace had totally freaked out.

It still freaked her out, but the way Tamara told it and the way Josh was laughing, she couldn't help but laugh too.

"So, which maze? What character did you get?" Josh asked after a minute.

"Candy Craze maze. Apparently, I'm playing Candy. I have no idea what that is," she said.

Suddenly, Josh stopped laughing and stared at her, eyes bulging. "Are you kidding me?"

"No, why?"

"You're playing Candy in Candy Craze?"

"Yes."

"And you don't know what that is?"

"No, why?" Candace said.

Suddenly, Josh started laughing again, so hard that he slid off the couch onto the ground where he clutched his sides as though in pain.

"What is it?" Candace asked, desperately wanting to be in on the joke.

"You're playing yourself," he gasped.

"Myself?"

"Yes."

"You mean?" Tamara asked, laughing too.

"Yes!"

Then they were both on the floor laughing. Candace stared at them in frustration. "What are you talking about?"

"You remember when you were trapped overnight in The Zone a few weeks ago?" Josh asked.

Of course she remembered. She didn't think she would ever forget that night. She and Kurt had been accidentally locked inside overnight. They had had their first big fight and broken up. Candace had been upset that he was a high school dropout with no plans for the future. They had gotten back together later on, but that night had been a terrible one. "Yeah, not forgetting that any time soon," she said.

"And you remember the urban legend that started to pop up afterward?"

"You mean that a psycho killer chased me through the park all night?" Candace asked.

Josh nodded.

"So?" she urged.

"They based the new maze on that urban legend. A psycho killer is loose in a deserted theme park, and he's chasing a terrified cotton candy operator through the maze. Her name is Candy."

She stared at him in horror, the full impact of what he was saying hitting her. "I'm playing myself," she whispered.

"That's what Josh said a minute ago," Tamara reminded her.

"This isn't funny," Candace told them.

They stared at her for a moment in silence before bursting out in even harder laughter.

"Yes, it really is," Tamara assured her.

Candace tried to decide which was more humiliating: the fact that she was playing herself in a fictitious version of her life or that they made her look like a floozy. She was standing in the costume department of The Zone on Saturday morning, looking at her reflection in a full-length mirror. The skirt was way shorter than the one she had worn all summer and had a tear in it revealing even more leg. Similarly, the blouse was slightly lower cut with several torn parts smeared with fake blood.

"You have got to be kidding me," she said as she did a slow spin.

"You think this is bad, you should see what I lobbied against," one of the costuming ladies told her. "The maze designers would have had you in your underwear."

"You're kidding!"

"Only a little. It wasn't underwear, but it was indecent at any rate. It's going to be hard enough spending several hours a night running in this getup."

"I'm not sure I can do this," Candace said.

"Play yourself. I figure if you can't laugh at yourself, life isn't worth it. Give it a try. You'd be surprised at what you can do."

Candace stared dubiously at the woman before adjusting her name tag that said Candy. "I guess it's true that the more things change, the more they stay the same," she sighed.

She had definitely planned to not have anything to do with cotton candy ever again, and yet here she was, playing a victimized cotton candy vendor.

"Janet, could I get some help?" someone shouted from one of the dressing rooms.

"Stay here, I'll be right back," Janet instructed.

Candace turned back to the mirror and stared at herself for a moment. Suddenly, the images of two men were reflected behind her, one on either side.

"Ummm … tasty," the taller of the two muttered.

"Makes me want candy," the other added in a voice that made Candace's skin crawl.

She turned to face the two men who both leered at her. "Who are you?" she demanded.

"I'm Will. This here is Brandon," the taller one said.

"We're what you'd call professional Scare monsters," Brandon added.

Professional creeps is more like it. Candace glanced toward the dressing rooms and wondered when Janet would reappear.

"This is our tenth year working Scare," Will said. "And you know why?"

"No," Candace said, taking a step backward.

"Because we like it," Brandon breathed, his hand descending on her shoulder.

Candace swallowed her own fear and prepared to knee him in the groin like her father had taught her when she was younger. She took a deep breath, ready to shout for help first. Before she could, Josh appeared.

"Knock it off, guys. Save your scare tactics for the players," Josh said.

Candace and the two men turned to look at him. Josh's tone was carefree as usual. He sounded like surfer Josh. But something in the way he held himself, though, was distinctly different. He looked taller somehow, and Candace had never noticed before just how broad his shoulders were.

Candace thought the white shirt of his vampire costume showed off the musculature of his upper body and made him seem more imposing than when he was wearing his normal tank top. It wasn't his shirt, she realized finally. It was the fact that he actually *seemed* dangerous. She found herself believing that he could rip both Will and Brandon apart with his bare hands and never break a sweat.

Brandon and Will must have felt it too. They beat a hasty retreat.

"No offense, miss," Will said.

"Sorry, dude," Brandon added.

Then the two were gone, and Candace sagged in relief. Josh stood for a moment, his posture still tense. Finally, he relaxed and turned to her.

"Sorry about that. I met those guys last year. They can be a little enthusiastic when it comes to scaring people, sometimes inappropriately so."

"They scared me," she admitted. "I'm so glad you came when you did."

"Janet's been working on my costume. She told me you were over here, so I came to show you what I've got so far. Pretty cool, huh?" he asked, spinning.

"Very nice," she said, her voice a little shaky. "I think you're missing the cape and fangs, though."

"Janet's still working on those."

"I don't know. You look more handsome than scary."

"That's the idea," he said, trying to look suave. "Seriously, thanks."

"No problem," she blushed slightly as she realized what she had said. "So, in which maze are the evil twins working? Not mine, I hope," she said.

"Nah. Horrific History, I think."

"That's the one Kurt's working."

"Good, he can keep an eye on him. Are you going to be okay?"

She nodded. "I'm still rattled, but I'll be okay."

"You want me to talk to a supervisor and see if I can get them fired?"

She wanted to say yes. Ultimately, though, that wouldn't help her face the jerks. She shook her head. "No, it'll be fine."

"Okay. By the way, love your costume."

She punched him in the arm.

"What was that for?"

"This is a terrible costume. I feel like I'm being exploited," she said, turning back to the mirror. "I can't believe they've made a maze out of this. I can't believe I'm starring in it."

"Very few people have had the impact on this park that you have," Josh said. "You should be proud."

"Proud is not the word I would use."

Janet finally returned. "That was quite a vanishing act," she chided Josh. "I turned to get your cape, and when I turned back you were gone."

"Sorry," he said, looking sheepish.

Janet attached the cape. Josh turned slowly, the cape fluttering. "Better?" he asked.

"Much," Candace said. "Which maze are you in, Count?"

"Why, Castle Dracula, of course," he said.

"Seriously?"

"Yup. It's in the castle. Haven't you been to a Scare before?"

"No," Candace admitted.

"Oh you should. It's marvelous fun," Janet said, fussing some more with Candace's costume.

"Truth be told, I'm terrified of mazes. I'm not too fond of being scared either," Candace said.

"Wow. This must be your idea of just the best time ever," Josh said.

Candace rolled her eyes. "I'm not sure how I let you talk me into it."

"Me? You're going to blame me?" he asked.

"Well, I can't very well blame Janet."

"Thank you. I get enough blame this time of year," Janet said, putting some pins around the bottom of Josh's cape.

"Who's getting blamed for what?" a familiar voice asked.

Candace turned and saw Roger, one of the guys who had been on her team for the end-of-summer scavenger hunt at the park. She gave him a quick hug.

"Hey, Roger, how's it going?" Josh asked.

"Great. I'm on the soccer team at school. Varsity," Roger said, pride in his voice.

"That's wonderful!" Candace said.

Before Scavenger Hunt, Roger had been the referee best known for tripping over his own feet. Winning that night had changed all of them, though, and Roger had gotten a much needed boost of confidence. Apparently, his klutziness was a thing of the past.

"So, are you back to be a maze monster?" Josh asked.

"Yeah, I get to be a dead baseball player in the Last Draft maze in the Game Zone."

"Stellar," Josh said, giving him a high five. "I'm Count Dracula."

"I was hoping so," Roger joked. "Otherwise we were going to have to talk about the whole cape thing. It works for you. I'm just not sure you want to adopt it as an everyday thing."

Josh laughed. "And what do you think of Candy?" he asked.

Roger turned and looked at her. "Are you actually playing yourself?" he asked.

"Apparently," she said.

"That's funny. Bold choice."

"I didn't exactly choose it. I got the part because I can scream really well."

There was a pause, and then Roger said, "Of course you can."

Janet left briefly and returned with a tattered and faded Yankees uniform, which she handed to Roger. His face lit up as he took it from her. "This is going to be great," he said. "I came to Scare once when I was twelve. I've been afraid to ever since."

"Didn't like the monsters?" Candace guessed.

"No, I knocked down twenty people and part of a maze roof," Roger said.

Candace bit her lip to keep from laughing, but it was no use.

🍁

Later that night Candace and Tamara were on Tamara's bed, talking. Candace had told her all about her day, and Tamara had laughed when she heard what happened to Roger at his first Scare.

"Promise me I won't embarrass myself that badly," Tamara gasped.

"I can't even promise I won't embarrass myself. I refuse to make any guarantees about you."

"Well, maybe if I do, Josh will swoop in and rescue me," Tamara teased.

"Are you sure you're not into him?" Candace asked.

"Yes. Like I told you, it's just not right."

"Okay, so he's not Mr. Right."

"No."

"How do you think you'll know when you meet Mr. Right?" Candace asked.

Tamara flipped onto her back. "I think it will hit me. You know, like magic, right between the eyes. Bam! There he'll be, and I'll just know."

"Don't you believe in love growing slowly? Like some people who start out as friends, or who kind of like each other and it grows deeper?" Candace asked. She would like to think that what she felt for Kurt could turn into love. She had to admit that as crazy as she was about him, she was pretty sure it wasn't love. At least, not yet. Maybe someday.

"I think that could happen for you, but not for me. I need to be shocked. You need to be surprised," Tamara said.

"Okay, you lost me. I don't get the difference," Candace confessed.

"Shock is sudden, jolting. It makes everything stop and then start again. You know, like an electric shock. I think it's going to take something that dramatic to get my attention and to tell me that he's the one. It'll be like I've always known it was him. I just never knew who he was until the moment I saw him."

Candace smiled. It sounded like Tamara. She had always been more impulsive, more dramatic than Candace.

"And surprised?" Candace asked.

"Surprise doesn't have to be harsh like shock. I'm thinking when you fall in love, you'll wake up one day and realize that it's been happening and you didn't even know it. It'll take you by surprise, but like a nice surprise, like getting a really great present for your birthday that you didn't expect."

"I have to admit, that sounds much nicer than shock," Candace said.

"And that is exactly why you'll be surprised and I'll be shocked."

Candace yawned and glanced at the clock. It was nearly two in the morning. "I'll be surprised *and* shocked if I can wake up in time for church."

Tamara hit her with a pillow. "Make fun now, but mark my words. One day you're in for the surprise of your life."

"Before or after you get the shock of yours?"

4

As it turned out, Candace made it to church on time, but she slunk low in the pew the entire time, trying to avoid looking at people from youth group. She still wasn't comfortable with the idea of them coming to see her at Scare. She dragged Tamara out as soon as the service was over.

They spent the rest of the day hanging out with Tamara's family, which was fun. The whole experience gave Candace a taste of what it would be like to have a sibling. She was disappointed when the weekend came to an end.

On Monday Candace made it through all of her classes without spending too much time worrying about her friends showing up to Scare. She had more immediate stress. She and Tamara had drama last period. The first week of school the instructor had been sick so they had study hall instead. Now class would really start, and Candace wasn't sure she was ready to be in the spotlight, no matter what Tamara said.

In the auditorium Candace and Tamara found two chairs side by side in the semi-circle in front of the stage. They sat down, and Candace looked around. She and Tamara were the only seniors in the class. *All the better to embarrass ourselves*, she thought.

Everyone took a seat, the bell rang, and Candace looked around for their teacher. Suddenly, Mr. Bailey appeared, somersaulting through the curtains to center stage.

Next to her, Tamara jumped, and Candace tried not to laugh. Tamara hated to be frightened. Maybe in some way this class would be harder on Tamara than her. It was at least something to hope for.

The teacher leapt to his feet and spread his arms wide. "I love the smell of fear in the afternoon," he joked. "My dear students, I am your teacher Mr. Bailey. Welcome to the theater."

Everyone cheered, except Tamara. She still looked uneasy from the initial scare.

Candace, on the other hand, had to give him style points for managing to twist a movie and a television quote and put them both together. Mr. Bailey bowed deeply and then sat down on the edge of the stage, his unnaturally long legs dangling.

"This is drama. This class is not for the fainthearted. I warn you now so that those of you who wish can flee."

Nervous laughter came from several people in the group.

"However, for those of you who wish to stay, I can open your mind and expand your horizons. And I promise you, you'll have fun doing it.

"Now, I realize that this is technically our first day of class. On the first day of class you expect to be given a syllabus and have the teacher explain how the class works, what kind of tests and papers you can expect, etc. However, this is drama, and the first rule is to expect the unexpected."

He sprang to his feet effortlessly. "I need a volunteer."

"Candace," Tamara piped up.

"What? No!"

"Candace it is. Candace, if you would be so kind as to join me on the stage," Mr. Bailey said.

Candace stood up, glaring daggers at Tamara. She looked at the stage for a moment in loss.

"You may either jump up here," Mr. Bailey said, "or take the stairs at the side of the stage," he indicated with a flourish.

Candace opted for the stairs.

"A sensible young lady," Mr. Bailey said by way of comment. "Let us see if we can change that."

The class laughed, and Candace trudged up the stairs in misery. Soon she was standing next to her teacher in the center of the stage. He was tall, well over six feet, and incredibly skinny. She had the impression that if she pushed on him just hard enough, he would topple over.

"Candace, you are going to help me demonstrate a little bit of improvisational theater. Just do as I tell you."

"Okay."

"Cluck like a chicken."

Candace hesitated for a moment and then did her best chicken cluck.

"Not bad. Now, flap your wings like a chicken."

Candace tucked her hands under her arms and flapped them up and down as though they were wings.

"Good. Now act like you're wiping your feet on a welcome mat. Wipe them hard, get everything off them."

She did as he told her, realizing that it was probably the same scratching motion that chickens made.

"Very good. Now ... be a chicken!"

She clucked and flapped and scratched all at the same time.

"Excellent! Watch out, the butcher's coming!"

She turned and ran back toward the stairs.

"Bravo! Thank you, Candace, you may take your seat. And that, class, is what we call improv."

Candace sat down.

"That was cool!" Tamara whispered.

"Just wait until you have to go up there," Candace said.

"Now that we have the unexpected out of the way," Mr. Bailey said, "we can move on to the expected." He jumped onto the ground and retrieved a stack of papers from a chair set off to the side. "This is your syllabus."

"You mean I was the only one who had to embarrass myself today?" Candace burst out before she could stop herself.

"Yes, and you did it beautifully," Mr. Bailey said with a smile.

Candace groaned and slid down in her chair.

They spent the next half hour going over the class rules and expectations. When it was over, Mr. Bailey made a final announcement. "I've been asked to remind any seniors in the class that you need to go to the office to sign up for your meetings with the guidance counselor. Good luck with that. And until tomorrow, so long, farewell, *auf Wiedersehen*, good-bye."

"Nice touch, ending with a quote from a musical," Tamara said.

"I'm still mad at you," Candace said.

"Don't be. You'll never have a first time to get up on that stage again. The rest of us are scared about what we'll have to do first. You can just relax since the worst of it is over."

"Okay, I acknowledge the soundness of your logic, and therefore I forgive you."

"Knew you would."

"Let's go get signed up for our meetings."

"Right behind you."

Ten minutes later they left the office and retrieved the stuff they needed from their lockers before heading for the parking lot.

"I'm betting the meeting with the guidance counselor will be a huge waste of time," Tamara said.

"I hope not. I'm hoping he can help me figure a couple of things out."

"Like what?"

"Like where to go to college, first of all."

"Somewhere around here. Maybe Cal State."

"Maybe, but there are a lot of colleges to choose from. Maybe I'd be better off somewhere else."

"Don't even joke about that. You are not allowed to move away to college," Tamara said.

"Why not?"

"Because I'm staying here, and I'll be devastated if you go."

Candace was distressed. "Well, I mean who knows? Besides, if I moved away, you could come visit and that would be totally awesome."

"No, both of us going to Cal State would be awesome," Tamara said.

"I'm kinda surprised you don't want to move away to college," Candace said.

"Why?"

"Well, you're the adventurous one. It just seems like more your style."

Tamara laughed. "I'm only adventurous in some areas of my life. Others I like to be nice, quiet, and stable."

Candace thought about that as she climbed into Tamara's car. It did make a certain amount of sense. Tamara didn't like surprises, and she usually classified change as a surprise. That was probably part of the reason she had flipped out when Candace got the summer job. It was at least something to think about.

"Hey, can we swing by The Zone? I want to pick up my new employee ID and stuff."

"Only if we can go on a ride."

"Your choice."

"Cool. I'm loving this season pass I got over the summer."

"Season ticket," Candace corrected before she could stop herself.

Tamara just laughed.

It only took Candace a couple of minutes to pick up her things. Then she and Tamara headed into the park to ride Rim-shot, one of the smaller, wilder roller coasters in the Thrill Zone.

Halfway there, Tamara stopped and pointed toward one of the stores. In the window was a Halloween display of new Scare merchandise. "Let's check it out."

Candace followed Tamara inside the store and looked at the mugs, antenna balls, and key chains on display. Tamara was rifling through the T-shirt racks. Suddenly she started laughing.

"What is it?" Candace asked.

"I think you have to have this," Tamara said, pulling a black T-shirt out and showing it to Candace. On the front in green letters that apparently glowed in the dark, it said, I Survived the Candy Craze! Tamara flipped it around so that Candace could get a look at the back. There was a picture of a girl in a cotton candy vendor outfit, looking up and screaming in horror as a knife descended toward her.

Candace grabbed the shirt and took a closer look. "Is that me?" she asked, horrified.

"Same hair, same eyes. I'm thinking yes."

"But they can't do that!"

"It's not an actual picture of you. They'll claim it's just an artist rendering of a generic girl."

"But—"

"I'm getting this for you."

"But—"

"Trust me, you'll thank me later. Just think. When Halloween is over, who better to say they survived the Candy Craze than you?"

The rest of the week seemed to fly by. It was uneventful except for an emergency run back home to get some more clothes. She also got her sleeping bag to take to the girls' all-night party at church. When she got the clothes back to Tamara's, she threw them in the wash to get rid of the stench of wet carpet, which seemed to have permeated nearly everything at the house.

Friday evening, Tamara and Candace loaded their stuff in the car and headed for church. "I love all-night parties," Tamara said.

"Remember last year?" Candace asked.

"When the guys tried to raid it and the neighbors saw them and called the police? That was so funny."

"And remember Tyler yelling that he wanted to make his one phone call?"

"I forgot about that! I thought that police officer was going to slap him," Tamara said.

"I wonder what's going to happen this year?"

"I hear Pastor Bobby ordered the guys not to raid the party this year," Tamara said.

"Yeah, but how many of them are going to listen?" Candace asked.

"To Pastor Bobby? A lot, I'll bet. He's cool, but I've seen him mad. Scary."

"I have a hard time picturing that."

"Trust me, girl, you don't want to see it."

They arrived at the church and parked next to the youth building. They hurried inside where two counselors and two dozen girls were trying to organize their stuff.

Candace recognized several senior girls as well as a couple of juniors. The rest were sophomores and freshmen, including the girl, Jen, who had asked what Scare was going to cost.

The pizzas were delivered shortly after they arrived, and everyone grabbed a slice and a soda and spread out on the floor. Jen approached Candace and Tamara and sat down by them, carefully balancing her pizza.

"I wanted to thank you for letting us all go to Scare," she said, looking at Candace.

Candace blushed. "I really had nothing to do with it. I'm just working there. You should thank Tamara. She's paying for everyone."

"Thank you," Jen told Tamara, her eyes wide and her face earnest. "I'm really excited. I've never been to anything like that before."

"That makes three of us," Tamara said. "It should be fun."

Other people overheard them and joined in the conversation. They all wanted to know what Candace was doing for Scare and how she had gotten the job.

"You seriously got it because you can scream really loudly?" Kim, a junior, asked.

"Yup."

"Let's hear," Joy urged.

"You'll hear at Scare," Candace said.

"Come on, do it now," another begged.

Suddenly everyone was asking her to demonstrate the scream that had gotten her hired. Candace hesitated, but Tamara poked her in the ribs. "Go on, let them have it."

Candace stood up. "Okay, but don't say I didn't warn you." She threw back her head and gave the loudest, most piercing scream she possibly could. When she stopped, she looked around the room. Everyone was staring in amazement. Somewhere in the distance she could hear dogs barking and howling.

"I bet they heard that a mile away," Jen said in awe.

Shannon, Pastor Bobby's fiancée, sighed heavily. "And I was so hoping the police weren't going to show up this year."

5

Candace kept telling herself that dress rehearsal was just that and nothing that she should be worried about. Still, that didn't help the school day go by any faster or make her feel any more confident.

Even once school was out, she felt like she was going to go crazy waiting for six-thirty when she could show up and get into costume. She completed her homework but wasn't very confident in the finished product. A math problem that should have taken her one minute ended up taking ten. She tried to lie down on the bed, but she couldn't get comfortable. Her parents had let her know that they'd be able to move back home in two days. That meant she would at least get a good night's sleep before Scare started.

Tamara drifted in and out, trying half a dozen times to engage Candace in conversation, but Candace was too nervous to talk much. Finally at about five thirty, Tamara came back in the room.

"Okay, your pacing is driving me crazy."

"Sorry," Candace apologized.

"Let's just head over there. So what if you're early? Besides, we can get some burgers on the way."

"You think so?"

"I know so. Anything is better than listening to you wear a hole in the carpet."

"Thanks, Tam."

"No problem."

Half an hour and a double cheeseburger and large fries later, Tamara parked in The Zone's employee lot.

"Call me when you need to be picked up."

"Thanks, you're the best," Candace said.

"Just remember, you're going to be great. Just relax and have fun."

"I'll try."

"Who's going to be here anyway?"

"From what I understand, management types walk through all the mazes and check it all out. I think the Game Masters who created them are supposed to be here too."

"If I say 'just be yourself' will you smack me?" Tamara asked with a smirk.

"No, but I'll scream," Candace threatened.

"Then never mind. I've heard you scream, and I don't think my eardrums could take it inside a closed car."

Candace got out of the car and hurried to the employee entrance. She showed the guards there her gate pass and stepped into the off-field world of The Zone. From there it only took her five minutes to reach the costuming department.

Looking at the number of people swarming around outside, Candace was grateful that Tamara had suggested she come early. She squeezed through the door of the building and crossed to the costume racks labeled CANDY CRAZE.

There were several seemingly identical costumes hanging there that must represent the psycho killer. It would make sense to have more than one in the maze in order to keep the action moving. Among the dark grays of those costumes, the pink and white of her cotton candy vendor uniform stood out all the more. She pulled it off the rack and got in line for one of the changing rooms.

All around her were lots of other people who were wearing bicycle shorts and T-shirts and were pulling their costumes on over them. *I should have thought to get a pair of black bicycle shorts to wear under this*, she thought, looking at her costume. It certainly would make her feel a little more comfortable, especially considering the slits in the skirt. She promised herself that she would get some the next day so she'd have them for opening night.

There was a great sense of energy in the building. The air practically pulsed with it. It reminded her a little bit of everyone waiting at the starting line for the end-of-summer scavenger hunt.

She looked around in fascination, trying to take it all in. There were mad scientists, vampires, aliens, ghosts, and freakish fairy tale creatures that were the more disturbing for their twists on familiar characters. A guy walked past her in a black leotard painted all over with fluorescent polka dots. Two dead gunfighters faced off against each other mockingly, while Lizzie Borden sat in a corner, admiring her axe. The headless horseman was tossing his pumpkin up and down, catching it one-handed.

Others were taking care of a fascinating variety of Scare props. Characters weren't allowed to touch players, but it was obvious they intended to work around this rule with props. One mummy dangled loose bandages over the heads of others nearby. Characters dressed as wax figures taunted and tormented each other with long feathers.

Suddenly a guy in a hockey mask slammed a tin can with a couple of coins in it against the wall near Candace's head, causing her to jump. Fortunately she managed not to scream. She watched in fascination as he went around the room, startling as many as he could with the noisemaker. She couldn't help but wonder who it was under the mask. She'd heard somewhere that almost sixty percent of the Scare people were full-time and seasonal employees. The other forty were made up of people like Will and Brandon who only worked Scare.

Someone tapped her on the shoulder, and she turned to see Roger, face pale and eyes sunken looking. He was holding a hanger with his baseball costume. She blinked a couple of times, amazed at just how ghostlike he looked.

"Wow!"

"Cool, huh?"

"Yeah."

"I just got out of the makeup chair. It took the woman half an hour. Now I have an overwhelming urge to scratch my nose and I can't."

"Bummer," she said.

"Tell me about it."

Candace had reached the front of the line, and a changing room had freed up. "Catch you later," she told Roger.

Five minutes later she was done, and she left the changing room with her street clothes in a bundle under her arm. She found herself in yet another line, this time to be checked over by Janet, the head of costuming.

When Candace finally reached the front of that line, she was directed to put her things on the floor and step up in front of a full-length mirror. Candace stared at herself while Janet walked around doing a final inspection.

"You look great, kid. Break a leg," Janet said at last.

Candace took one last look at herself in the mirror before turning away. The costume area was getting more crammed by the minute. Candace scooped up her clothes and headed for the Locker Room, which was the name for the employee storage area.

She had no sooner locked up her stuff than Kurt walked in, took one look at her, and let out a whistle. "That one's better than your summer uniform," he said admiringly. "Except for the fake blood."

"Too gross?" Candace asked.

He shook his head. "No, actually it's kinda hot . . . in a disturbing sort of way."

"Great, because that's what I need," she sighed.

Kurt was wearing black jeans, a black turtleneck, and black shoes. Umpires had to fade completely into the background. "Aren't you going to get hot wearing that?" she asked.

He nodded. "Although it's not as bad as you might think. Umpires don't have to move around much, so it ends up being better than most of the costumes."

"Too bad we're not working in the same maze," she pouted.

He pulled her into his arms for a quick kiss and then let her go.

"Like I said, too bad we're not working in the same maze," she said.

He winked at her. "You'll be okay. Just don't let any of the other umpires kiss you."

"I wouldn't dream of it."

"Yeah, but they certainly would," he said, looking her over again.

She blushed. "Stop. You're embarrassing me."

He laughed. "Come on, I have just enough time to walk you to your maze before I have to report at mine."

They walked out into the park as the last light was leaving the sky. It was weird seeing the park practically deserted at that time of day, and Candace shivered as she recalled for a moment how it had felt the night she and Kurt got trapped in the park.

"You cold?" he asked.

"No, just nervous."

"You're going to be great. After all, it is your maze. You are Candy."

"That's what I'm afraid of," she muttered.

The Candy Craze maze had been erected in the middle of the Holiday Zone. Some of the mazes in the park were created in existing buildings. The Mummy's Curse wound through the Tomb of the Pharaohs in the Egypt area, and the House of Wax took over the House of Cards in the Game Zone. Some mazes took over a cluster of buildings, like the Haunted Village, which took over the Seaside Village shops and buildings in the Splash Zone. Others, like the Last Draft, were constructed with sturdy plywood in the middle of open spaces.

The Candy Craze was one of the latter types—with a twist. It had been created in the open spaces in and around the Holiday Zone. Some of the normal rides had been incorporated into the maze to make it really feel like an abandoned amusement park. A huge sign over the entrance blazed the words Candy Craze in four-foot-tall neon letters. The sign was the only thing that didn't look decayed and dilapidated.

Candace hovered on the threshold, her fear of mazes gnawing at her mind. "I'm not sure I want to go in there," she told Kurt.

"Of course you don't want to," an unfamiliar female voice said.

Candace jumped and turned to see the speaker, a blonde woman in a gray business suit with a name tag that said Tish. She looked to be in her thirties. She held a clipboard in her left hand and was wearing a headset.

"It's dark in there," the woman continued. "Dangerous too. Anyone can tell that. Everything inside you tells you not to venture into the abandoned amusement park where sinister things might be lurking. And yet you will. They all will, because they can't help themselves. They just have to know," the woman finished, her voice fervent.

"Wow," Candace said, not sure what else would be appropriate to say at the moment.

"Wow indeed. That's why they'll be lining up to walk through here. Thousands of them."

"Who are you?" Candace asked finally.

The woman seemed to come out of whatever trance she was in, and she looked directly at Candace for the first time.

"I'm Tish Morgan. I'm the Game Master in charge of developing this maze." She held out her hand, and Candace shook it.

"I'm Candace."

"Better known as Candy," Kurt said, clearing his throat.

Tish's eyes widened. "It's you!" she squealed.

"Yeah, it's me," Candace said.

"Well, of course it is," Tish said, suddenly hugging her tight. "What a brave, brave girl you are. And if it wasn't for you, we wouldn't have the most amazing new maze ever!"

"Yeah, but—" Candace said, struggling to breathe.

"But nothing. It's you, all you. You're amazing. Why, if it had been me, I don't know if I could have done what you did."

"I really didn't do anything," Candace said.

Tish hushed her and was suddenly talking on her headset. "Get a photographer over to the Candy Craze maze stat! You'll never believe who we got to play Candy!"

She held up a finger to indicate that she'd be back with Candace in a minute and then moved a few feet away to continue her conversation. "I know, isn't it fabulous? We have to get some publicity photos."

"I think I should call my lawyer," Candace muttered.

"And by that you mean your dad, right?" Kurt asked.

"Yeah. I don't think I want them taking my picture."

"Come off it," Kurt said. "This is a big deal! Exciting! People want to fawn over you. Let them."

"I'm not sure I'm comfortable—"

Kurt waved a hand to cut her off. "Comfortable has nothing to do with it, Candace. If you wanted to be comfortable, you should have stayed home and never gotten a job in the first place. Live life or go hide, it's up to you."

She felt like she'd just been slapped. A thousand angry retorts crowded her mind. Before she could give voice to any of them, though, Kurt glanced at his watch.

"I gotta run or I'm going to be late. See you," he said, before turning and jogging off toward the History Zone.

"See you," Candace said to his back. As the angry retorts faded, they were replaced with a sense of bewilderment. What could she have said to push Kurt's buttons like that?

She didn't have long to think about it because a photographer arrived. The photographer and Tish dragged Candace all over the maze, posing her this way and that as he took pictures. By the time they were finished, several of the referees playing the psycho killer had showed up. Then the photographer had a field day posing Candace with various ones.

At last the photographer retreated, and a couple other people wearing suits showed up along with all the umpires. Tish led them all through the maze first, pointing out where the various umpires would be stationed. Candace had to admit that the dark, empty rides and the general sense of decay were extra creepy. If The Zone had looked like this the night she was trapped in it, she probably would have been convinced killers were lurking around every corner.

Once they had walked the maze once, including the exits that were only to be used by referees, the umpires took up their positions. Tish and two of the men with her positioned the psychos throughout the maze, giving them props and directions. They saved Candace for last.

"Okay. This maze is all about you, dear Candy," Tish said. "We want the players to experience your fear as if it were their own. We also want them to be able to watch you running in terror from the killer."

"Okay."

"You're good at screaming?"

"It's what got me the job," Candace said with a smile.

"Good, good. Now, let me walk you through this."

Together they entered the maze again. The hall went straight for twenty feet and then turned sharply to the left. On the right-hand side was a small alcove where one of the psychos was already waiting.

"Unlike most of our mazes, we're only going to send guests through in groups of ten to fifteen. This will increase the wait times, but we felt it was worth it if we could replicate for the players your sense of isolation," Tish said.

"Each group will come down this hall. Before they get to the corner, you're going to run, screaming across their path, and he's going to chase you," Tish said, indicating the psycho.

"Now, instead of going straight, you'll duck behind this curtain on your left," Tish said, showing it to her. "When the players come around this corner, they'll be startled because they won't see you. However, once they pass the curtain, your pursuer will jump out and chase them down this next hallway."

"And what do I do?" Candace asked.

"You're going to move on to another scene a quarter of the way through the maze," Tish said, guiding her through the parts of the maze the players wouldn't see. "You can watch from here using this angled mirror, then you'll run past them again."

Candace nodded, checking the mirror.

"See, the idea is that each group will see you five times, including the finale where the psycho catches you."

"He catches me?"

"Yes. The players escape, but you are not so lucky."

Tish walked her through the maze, showing her where to run, hide, wait, and watch. At last they came to a scene with part of a crashed Ferris wheel on the ground. The final psycho was there, and they rehearsed him catching Candace and standing behind her with an arm around the upper part of her chest and shoulders as she screamed and struggled.

Candace was a little nervous, but the guy inside the suit—whose name was Ray—was really nice and gentle. They practiced the catch a dozen times until she felt comfortable with it.

"Okay, you think you have it?" Tish asked.

"I think so," Candace said.

"Great." Tish looked at her watch. "It's just about time for us to run through it all for our test audience. Take your place back at the front of the maze and get ready to go live."

Candace made her way fairly easily back to the beginning and waited there with psycho number one, whose name turned out to be Reggie. They had been in place for about three minutes when there was a sudden hissing and the hall started filling with fake fog.

Candace coughed as she breathed in her first lungful.

"It takes some getting use to," Reggie said.

Candace coughed again. Her lungs were trying to convince her that they didn't want to stick around long enough to get used to it. A minute after the fog started, the music kicked on. The beat was loud and pounding. Candace could swear that she could feel the walls vibrating. The song sounded familiar, but the pacing and the voice of the singer did not. Then in one horrific moment it hit her.

"Oh, please no," she groaned.

It was an acid rock version of "I Want Candy." It was the song that had driven her crazy all summer, every time she heard it in the Kids Zone. It worked though. For just a moment she was standing back there, summer sun plastering her hair to her forehead, the name tag Candy—that she could never get changed to Candace—pinned in place, and people lining up wanting nothing but sticky cotton candy.

Five minutes later Tish reappeared. She leaned in close and shouted to be heard over the music. "Okay, we've got our execs who are going to be the test audience outside and ready to go. We'll be sending them through in a minute, so get ready."

Candace gave her a thumbs-up. Tish disappeared back toward the exit, and Candace stood, heart pounding, fists clenching. It was the moment of truth. From where she was standing, she could see the hallway, but people coming down it couldn't see her.

She could feel Reggie tensing behind her. Then she saw the executives enter the maze. She waited until they were a few feet from the corner before springing out from her hiding space and running across their path. She was screaming, and Reggie was on her heels.

She almost missed the curtain they were supposed to duck behind, but Reggie grabbed her arm, which made Candace scream for real. The two ducked behind the curtain. Candace moved toward her next position while Reggie waited for the group to pass. He jumped out behind them and chased them down the hall.

Candace's next three dashes across the group's path went well, which just left the finale. By the time she got there, she was panting from stress and excitement. Ray caught her right on cue and spun her around, arm wrapped around her.

And that was when Candace got a good look at the test group. It was a mixed group of men and women, but it was the man in front who drew her eyes. It was none other than John Hanson, owner of the park.

For a moment Candace forgot to struggle, but then Ray nudged her, and she started kicking and screaming again. In response, the group started applauding. When they finished, they exited the maze and Ray released her.

"I think that went well," he said.

"How do you know?"

"They almost never applaud."

Candace ran back toward the front of the maze, not sure if there was another group that was going to be coming through. Fortunately, they had set up the maze so the entrance and the exit were right next to each other.

She made it back to her starting alcove. A minute later the music and the fog stopped. Tish walked through. "Great job, guys. See you on Friday," she told Candace and Reggie.

"So, we can go?" Candace asked.

"Yup. Get out of here."

6

Candace walked slowly out of the maze. She was exhausted. This worried her since she'd only been at work for an hour instead of seven. All she really wanted was to call Tamara to pick her up so she could crash. She didn't like the way Kurt had left things though.

She headed for the History Zone, hoping to catch Kurt before he left. Just as she entered that part of the park, people were streaming out. She could tell from the costumes they had to be coming from the Mummy's Curse. There were mummies, people with animal heads, and a guy who looked like he was being eaten alive by scarab beetles.

Suddenly one of the mummies collapsed onto the ground. Several people dropped down to check on the person. Someone in black clothes got on a walkie-talkie.

"We have a mummy down. I repeat, a mummy is down."

Candace bit her lip. Josh had warned her that every weekend at least one mummy fainted from the heat of the costume. This must be the first one, and Scare hadn't even started yet.

Suddenly the guy covered in scarab beetles noticed Candace. "Hey, look! It's Candy!" he said, pointing to her.

Several people came up to her, talking all at once.

"Wow, it's really you!"

"I'm so sorry about what happened. That must have been terrifying!"

"Kurt told me about how the psycho locked him in the bathroom. He said he could hear you screaming but couldn't come to help."

"Did the guy hurt you?"

"Wait, Kurt said what?" Candace asked, not sure if she had heard right and unclear who in the group had said it.

"All right, coming through!" a loud voice boomed.

Everyone turned to see paramedics with a stretcher. The group moved closer to the fallen mummy.

"Heat exhaustion," one of the paramedics said. "Happens every year."

"What did Kurt say?" Candace asked again. No one was listening though.

Candace shook her head and kept walking. Kurt couldn't really be helping spread the urban legend, could he?

She made it to the entrance of the Horrific History maze just in time to catch Kurt as he was leaving.

"Hey, there's my Candace!" he said brightly, as though nothing had happened earlier.

"Hey," she said.

"How'd it go?" he asked.

"Good, but I'm exhausted already. I can't imagine how I'm going to survive the weekend."

"It's amazing how much adrenaline can help with that. Once people are running through the mazes laughing and screaming, it will give you a boost. You'll probably sleep half of Monday, but I guarantee you'll make it through the weekend."

"I hope so."

"It's going to be an awesome year, I can tell. Everyone's already really excited. Your maze is incredible. It will have them lining up halfway across the park."

"About that. Kurt, did you tell people that there really was a psycho killer who chased me through the park?" she asked.

"No. Other people told me that," he said with a smile.

"Did you tell them it wasn't true?"

"I tried, but gave up. People would rather believe it's true."

"So, what did you tell them?" she asked.

"I might have said that the psycho locked me in one of the bathrooms so that I couldn't come to your aid."

"You didn't!"

He smiled impishly. "And it's possible I said that I could hear you screaming but couldn't crawl out of the window because it was too small."

"Kurt! How could you lie like that?!" she asked, amazed.

"And it was probably me that mentioned that I broke my arm trying to batter down the door."

She stared at him in disbelief. Now it was easy to see why she was fighting a losing battle in proclaiming the truth. For every truth she told, Kurt told a lie, and so the legend only grew.

"You're not helping, you know."

"What? People are going to believe it anyway. All I'm doing is adding a little flavor, making it a little more interesting. That's all. A year from now people won't even be able to link it to us. Might as well have fun with the urban legend while we can."

"You are unbelievable! Forget the fact that you're lying, how can you stand to draw that much attention to yourself?"

"Hello? Look what I do for a living. What's a little more attention?"

"Okay, fine. But please think about me. I really don't want or need this kind of attention. I'm tired of being stared at and talked about and questioned about things that never hap- pened. It's humiliating!"

"Candace, I'm sorry you feel that way. Really I am."

"So, will you stop helping the story along?"

"No."

What could she say to that? She just stared at him, wondering if there was anything anyone could say to change his mind. She thought wildly of trying to get her father to get an injunction that would keep Kurt from talking about those things. However, that was only likely to draw even more unwelcome attention.

"Sorry," he said.

She turned and walked away, not trusting herself to say anything to him at that moment. She was angry and profoundly disappointed.

"Candace, you okay?"

She turned and saw Becca. The other girl was dressed up like a pirate and walking with some of the others from the Muffin Mansion. Becca separated from the group and came to a stop by Candace.

"I'm mad at Kurt," Candace blurted out without thinking.

"I'm sorry. What happened?"

"He's telling people that I really was chased around the park by a psycho killer. He's not helping me clear it up; he's feeding the fires of curiosity and making the legend more bizarre. I asked him to stop, and he won't."

Becca put her hand on Candace's shoulder. "That stinks. Try and see it from his point of view though."

"And that would be what exactly?"

"When else is Kurt in his entire life going to have the chance to be this famous?"

"What?" Candace asked. "What does that have to do with anything?"

"Everything actually. For right now, the story is exciting. Everyone wants to hear about it, and he gets to be famous. I'm sure he's also adding little touches to make himself sound heroic too."

"He's claiming he broke his arm trying to break down a bathroom door to save me."

"See? When will he ever get to be that kind of hero in real life?"

"You never know," Candace said.

"Exactly. And neither does he. With guys, it's usually about ego. The story makes him feel important, special. He probably doesn't want anybody, including you, taking that away from him."

"But he's lying," Candace protested.

"Yeah. I'm not saying it's right. I'm just telling you what's probably going on inside his head."

On Friday morning Candace woke up with full-fledged butterflies in her stomach. She turned off her alarm and considered retreating back under her covers. It reminded her of how she had felt when she first went to work at The Zone. *Come on, Candace*, she lectured herself. *That turned out pretty well.*

She was at least grateful to finally be back home in her own bed. She'd had the best night's sleep she'd had in days. She dragged herself out of bed and got dressed. Then she headed downstairs to catch a ride from her mom. Tamara had some kind of appointment and had told Candace she couldn't give her a ride to school.

Candace found her mom in the kitchen, downing her morning cup of coffee. Her mom looked at her over the brim of the cup and said, "Nervous."

It wasn't a question, but a statement. Candace had known her mom long enough to tell the difference.

"Is it that obvious?" Candace asked.

Her mom nodded slowly, as though she didn't have enough caffeine running through her system to function fully yet.

"It's going to be okay though, right?" Candace asked.

"I don't know," her mom said.

Candace stared at her for a minute. "What do you mean?"

"I can't promise you everything is going to be okay. I don't know that it will."

"What happened to the standard 'everything will be okay'?" Candace asked.

Her mom shrugged. "You're practically an adult. You'll be eighteen in a couple of months. I think you're old enough for the truth."

Candace slumped. "I like the platitudes better," she grumbled.

"Don't we all," her mom said, draining the last of her coffee. "Ready to go?"

"No."

A few minutes later her mom dropped her at the corner by her school. As Candace trudged through the parking lot, she noticed Tamara's car. That was weird. She had assumed Tam would be missing homeroom for whatever it was she had to do.

"Way to go, Candace," a guy said, walking toward his car. He gave her double thumbs-up, and she smiled.

"Thank you," she said, not sure what he was praising her for.

A couple of freshmen giggled and waved to her. Candace waved back. "What is happening?" she said under her breath.

A moment later she spotted the first banner. At first glance it looked like any of the billboards around town advertising Scare. Looking closer, though, she saw what the difference was. There was a picture of her in her Scare costume.

She stumbled and nearly fell. As she stared in horror, the words underneath the photo came into focus. Come see senior Candace Thompson at her night job. Come tonight with Valley Church youth group and get in free! There was also a contact number to call for details.

"Tamara!" Candace hissed.

As though on cue, her friend appeared. "Surprise!" Tamara said, a huge grin on her face.

"How could you do this to me?" Candace asked.

"You pretty much did it to yourself," Tamara said. "I figured I'd just make sure you have a good opening-night crowd."

"But, but I don't want people I know to be there! First church and now school! I won't be able to show my face anywhere by the time you're through!"

"That's what friends are for," Tamara said.

"You keep saying that, but I don't think this is what friends are for," Candace said, gesturing toward the sign. A passing junior mistook the gesture and gave her a high five as he walked by.

"Look at that, you're famous. Now I'm the one in your shadow," Tamara laughed, clearly enjoying herself.

Candace wasn't going to be able to make Tamara see just how embarrassing the whole thing was. She stared at her friend in bewilderment. She knew that Tamara thought she was doing a good thing.

Let it go Candace. This can only end in tears, probably your own. She closed her eyes. *God, please help me to get through this without completely humiliating myself*, she prayed.

She heard a series of wolf whistles followed by a guy saying, "Way to go, Candace!"

So much for complete humiliation. She opened her eyes and squared her shoulders. "Let's get this day over with," she said.

By the time Candace made it to drama, she was exhausted. She had kept a fake smile plastered on all day and had answered dozens of questions, many from people she didn't even know. When the drama class gave her a standing ovation as she entered, she figured it was the crowning moment of the school day and did the only thing she could. She took a bow.

"I didn't think people got applause until after they performed," she joked.

"Depends on the circumstances," Mr. Bailey said.

Candace took her seat and was grateful that after the initial outburst, the class became less about her and more about improvisation. Better yet, when her turn came, she got to act out the role of an old man, which was as far from a cotton candy vendor as she could get.

The moment school let out, she called Kurt and told him what Tamara had done. Kurt just started laughing.

"It's not funny!" Candace protested.

"Sure it is. Besides, that's awesome. Just imagine, everyone you know will come see you."

She rolled her eyes in frustration as she realized she had chosen the wrong person to vent to. Kurt spent his days as a costumed character. He enjoyed showing off.

"This is completely humiliating," she said.

"Get over it. You'll be fine. And just imagine how cool this will make Scare for everyone who knows you. You should be happy that you're not wearing a mask. This way everyone will know who you are."

"Great," Candace said.

"It's going to be an awesome Scare. All the mazes look awesome."

"I haven't had a chance to look at them all," Candace admitted.

"You totally should. You're lucky, though, you're working in the coolest one. Candy Craze is going to draw the biggest crowds this year. Lines will probably be at least an hour long."

Maybe most of the people she knew would give up and head for the mazes with shorter lines. She could hope at least.

"Which is your favorite?" she asked Kurt.

"Well, obviously I have a soft spot for Candy Craze."

"I would hope so."

"But my favorite has got to be Tombstone in the Old West part of the History Zone. It's killer."

"Very funny."

"As far as the rides go, I think the River Styx overlay of the Odyssey boat ride is way cool."

Candace wondered if she would even have a chance to check out the rides, or if she would be way too busy with her

Scare duties. "So, when can I see you?" she asked. She winced as she said it. It sounded lame and needy, even to her.

"You might see me tonight. It depends on if our breaks match up," he said.

"That's not what I meant. I meant see you, as in date."

"Oh. Well, obviously the weekend's pretty booked. I've got classes Monday, Tuesday, and Wednesday evenings at the community college. I could maybe do an early dinner on Tuesday though. Say four thirty?"

"Sounds good," Candace said.

"Well, gotta run. Bye."

"Bye."

No sooner had she hung up than her phone rang. She looked at the caller ID and saw that it was Josh.

"Hey there," she said, answering the phone.

"Hey there yourself," Josh said. "How are you?"

"Completely humiliated," she said.

"Why, what happened?"

"Tamara plastered banners all around school inviting people out to Scare tonight. They featured a picture of me in costume."

"Ouch! Sorry. If I'd known why she wanted a picture of you in costume, I wouldn't have given it to her."

"So, you're the culprit!"

"Guilty. Forgive me?"

"You're forgiven. Sounds like you were a victim of her evil scheme too."

Josh laughed. "At least Tamara's being supportive. It could be a whole lot worse."

It could indeed. Over the summer Candace and Tamara had nearly lost their friendship when Tamara hadn't supported Candace in her need to get a summer job. She shuddered, not wanting to think what coming back to school would have been like if they hadn't worked out their problems.

"So, what's up?" she asked Josh, deciding to change the subject.

"I didn't know if you'd heard, but you'll want to get there half an hour early tonight for some group photos and general pep talks. Plus, it's nearly impossible to get a dressing room first night because everybody takes so long to fuss with their costumes."

"Thanks. I'll make sure and get there early." The butterflies she had been battling all day came back with a vengeance. "So, just how crazy is this going to be?"

Josh laughed. "It'll be a madhouse, and opening weekend usually has only half the number of players as the following weekends."

"Not this year, if Tamara has anything to say about it," Candace sighed.

"I know it's embarrassing, but it is really cool of her to pay for admission for all those people. I bet some of them have never gotten to attend something like Scare. It's fun, but it isn't cheap."

Candace thought about Jen from youth group who had looked so worried when she was asking how much Scare would cost. Josh was right. There were a lot of people at her church with money but just as many didn't have much of anything. Tamara was providing a special thing for a lot of people.

"Thanks, Josh."

"For what?"

"Helping me get some perspective."

"No problem. Catch you tonight, Candy."

She smiled at the nickname as she hung up.

Sitting on the bench out by the school parking lot, she bowed her head and prayed. *God, help me to do my best tonight, and help everyone who comes to have a good time and to be able to truly enjoy the evening and the companionship. Amen.*

She opened her eyes just as Tamara showed up in the parking lot. Tamara rushed over as Candace stood up. Tamara grabbed her arm and held it high above both their heads. "A celebrity is riding in my car!" Tamara shouted.

Candace groaned as heads turned.

Tamara gave a shout, and finally Candace joined her.

"This is awesome!" Tamara said at last.

Candace laughed. Maybe she had been taking the whole thing way too seriously. The point of Scare was to be crazy and to have fun. As they walked to Tamara's car, Candace joined her in shouting to everyone she could see, "Make sure you come to Scare!"

People waved, gave a thumbs-up and shouted encouragingly. Candace began to laugh in earnest. This had to be what being popular felt like.

7

As Candace arrived at The Zone, she desperately tried to hold on to her earlier enthusiasm and not get overwhelmed by the jitters. When she reached the costume department, the excitement in the air was double what it had been for dress rehearsal.

She saw Becca exit one of the dressing rooms in full pirate gear, and Candace feared she might be high on sugar. Becca was hopping slightly as she walked. Becca was allergic to sugar. It made her more than a little crazy, and uncontrollable hopping was definitely one of the symptoms.

"Hey, Candace!" Becca said, rushing over to her.

"You haven't been eating sugar, have you?" Candace asked.

"No. Do you have some?"

"No. Sorry."

"That's okay," Becca said, looking disappointed.

"So, the Muffin Mansion people are all going to be pirates?" Candace asked.

"Yup. It's going to be awesome. Although we're more privateers than pirates."

"What's the difference?" Candace asked.

"Pirates work for themselves. Privateers work for a king."

"But all the pillaging and plundering?" Candace asked.

"Oh, just as much as pirates, but there's a legal loophole for it all," Becca said smirking.

"Cool."

"Totally," Becca said with another little hop. "See you later."

Candace removed her costume from the rack and got in line for one of the dressing rooms.

"Well, well, if it isn't the newbie," she heard someone say.

She glanced to her left and saw Brandon and Will staring at her. They were both dressed in tattered costumes and had grotesque fake scars on their faces. Both of them wore black knee pads over their pants.

"What do you want?" she asked.

"Just a little Candy," Brandon said, leering at her.

"Grow up," she snapped.

They both laughed sadistically at that. "Grow up, grow up," Will mocked.

"I don't know, Will, are we ready to grow up?" Brandon asked.

"I'm not sure. Let me think. Nope!"

Will touched her shoulder, and Candace jerked away. "Get away from me!" she snapped.

Then she felt something touching the skin just below her throat. "What on earth?" she asked, moving her hand there.

She screamed when she touched something furry and moving. "Get it off me!" she shrieked.

"What's the matter, scared of a little mouse?" Brandon said.

The girl in front of Candace turned around and grabbed the mouse that was trying to get under Candace's hair. The girl held the mouse out to Will. "Keep your little friend to yourself or I'll squash him," she threatened.

Will snatched the mouse back. "There, there, she didn't mean it," he cooed to the thing.

Will and Brandon retreated, and Candace thanked the girl in front of her.

"Don't let those guys get to you," she said.

"I'll try. At least they're not working in my maze. I thought they were working in a history maze, but it doesn't look like it from their costumes."

"They're in one of the Scare zones that guests walk through between attractions. They run through the dark, slide on their knees, and try to scare people."

Candace shuddered. "That shouldn't be too hard for them."

A few minutes later Candace was dressed, and she headed for her maze. She still had half an hour to kill so she walked around admiring some of the other decorations and themes. Finally she headed back to her own maze and met up with the psychos mingling outside.

"This is the big night," someone who she thought was Ray said to her.

"Yeah. Have you worked one of these before?"

"This is my fourth year. Gets wilder each time. I've never been in the featured maze before though. We'll all have to work extra hard to live up to the reputation this maze already has."

"How can this maze already have a reputation when no one has gone through it?" Candace asked.

"You'd be surprised."

A supervisor showed up. "Places everyone!"

Candace was one of the last to walk into the maze. When she reached her alcove, Reggie was already there.

"I've got a lot of friends showing up tonight," Candace told Reggie.

"Does that make you nervous or excited?"

"Terrified."

"Join the club. That's one of the reasons I wanted to work as one of the psychos in this maze. Anonymity. My friends know I'm in here, they just don't know where."

"I'll have to remember that for next time," Candace said. *If there is a next time.*

The fog and music suddenly kicked on, and Candace jumped. A minute later a supervisor came walking through. "Ten minutes to show," he told everyone.

Candace's heart started pounding in earnest. For a moment she was terrified that she was going to pass out. That would probably be the worst thing she could do. Way more humiliating than running and screaming. Suddenly, fainting topped her list of anxieties about the evening.

"You'll be great," Reggie said encouragingly.

"Thanks. I'm sure you will be too."

And then there was movement at the entrance. There was no time to think. Candace jumped out and ran. The fog was a lot thicker than it had been at rehearsal, and she couldn't see the black curtain. She panicked when she realized she had missed it and glanced over her shoulder. Reggie was nowhere to be seen.

Candace sprinted down the hall as fast as she could, startling an umpire. She was desperate to get around the next turn before the players saw her alone in the hallway. She made it and somehow found her way to the next spot she was supposed to appear.

She saw the group coming and jumped out a second too late, ricocheting off the lead guy and spinning into the wall. She kept her feet under her, though, and kept running. When she reached the finale, she was relieved to discover that she didn't recognize anyone in the group. She returned to the start, determined not to mess up again.

Tamara was in the tenth group to come through. With her were several of the girls from youth group and one of the girls from Drama. Candace screamed especially loud, and they screamed back, obviously having practiced to do just that.

The next hour was a nightmare. Every group that came through was made up of people from church or school or both. Fortunately Candace was able to do everything right.

The rest of the night passed in a blur. By the time it was over and Candace turned in her costume, she was shaking with fatigue from head to toe.

"You okay?" Kurt asked, looking concerned.

She nodded. "I survived," she said, realizing that Tamara had been right to buy her the Candy Craze T-shirt.

"I heard you did more than that," he said. "I heard you rocked."

"I hope so."

"Get some rest. I'll see you tomorrow night."

"Okay," she said.

She made it to her car and called Tamara. She wanted someone to talk to while she was driving so she wouldn't fall asleep.

"Well?" she asked when Tamara picked up.

"Amazing!"

"Yeah?"

"Seriously, you were totally awesome!" Tamara shrieked.

"Thanks," Candace said, praying she could drive home in safety.

"Everyone can't stop talking about it. A bunch of us are still at the church if you want to come hang out."

"I'd love to, but I can barely keep my eyes open," Candace admitted.

Tamara instantly sounded sympathetic. "I believe it. I have no idea how you could keep that up all night."

The funny part was that Tamara and all the other players probably had done as much running and screaming as Candace had. At the end of the day, though, she guessed that the big difference between attending Scare and working it was that the excitement of being a player gives you energy for hours, while the ref just gets sweaty and stressed.

They talked for a couple of more minutes until Candace was nearly home.

"Call me tomorrow," Tamara said.

"I will," Candace promised.

She made it home. She staggered into her room and fell on her bed still in her clothes. She hugged Mr. Huggles, thought about putting on her pajamas, and fell asleep.

Slowly Candace began to wake up. Her throat felt scratchy, and her eyes were burning. Her body felt sore all over. It took her a minute to realize that she was probably suffering from the aftereffects of Scare. She started coughing and could swear she tasted the fake fog from the night before.

She rolled over and looked at her clock. It was eleven in the morning. At least she had gotten some sleep. She vaguely remembered falling asleep around four.

She staggered out of bed and, after a quick trip to the bathroom, changed into jeans and a T-shirt. She headed downstairs and was surprised to find her parents smiling at her from the kitchen table where a variety of food was waiting. She coughed for a moment and finally asked, "What's all this?"

"We call it brunch," her dad said, a twinkle in his eye.

"You guys should have woken me," she said and then promptly yawned.

"We figured you needed your rest. It was a big night last night. How did it go?" her mom asked.

"Good," Candace said, sliding into her chair. "I'm tired though. I never knew running and screaming could be so much work."

Both her parents laughed. "Well, when that's all you're doing for hours at a time, I imagine it would be exhausting," her dad said.

"Did you recognize anyone from youth group?" her mom asked.

Candace nodded. "I recognized everyone from youth group. I don't think anyone *didn't* come last night. Plus I saw at least fifty kids from school and dozens of kids I didn't know but I'm sure were part of the group. They all came through in a big group. Tamara said there were almost four buses full. They had to borrow a bus from the church next door."

"Well, that's wonderful! What a great outreach. I'm sure Pastor Bobby was pleased," her mom said.

Candace laughed. "Tamara said at one point Pastor Bobby started screaming so loud in one of the mazes that it scared everyone else and they stampeded for the exit."

Her father started laughing really hard at that. "That would have been something worth seeing."

Candace started laughing too. "Since I'm not one of the monsters, my job isn't to scare people, but I accidentally scared several."

"Tell us," her mom urged.

"I ran around a corner and right into this one guy. He was wearing gang colors, and he was there with six other guys."

"Were you hurt?" her father asked, instantly concerned.

"No, but I scared him so badly that he fell down on the ground and started screaming like a little girl. All his friends started laughing so hard at him that they were crying. I was laughing too, but I had to keep running. I was laughing and screaming at the same time, and it was so hard!"

As they ate brunch, Candace told her parents about the other funny things that had happened. She ran out of stories at the same time she ran out of appetite. Her mother got up to start clearing dishes, and her father leaned close.

"We are very proud of you, Candace."

"Thanks, Dad."

"It is good to see you really put your heart into something. I think The Zone has been very good for you."

"Thanks," she said, blushing slightly. It pleased her to hear him say that, but it also shamed her slightly when she thought about how much she complained about her work.

Her mom returned to the table. "We're planning on coming to Scare tonight to see you," she said.

"Really? That would be great!" Candace said, standing up to give her mom a quick hug.

"We figured there was already enough pressure on you last night and it would be better if we waited until tonight," her dad explained.

"This will be great. Now I have someone to perform for tonight too," she said with a laugh.

It was funny to think that just a day earlier that thought would have terrified her. She started coughing again and grimaced. It turned out the only bad thing about working Scare was breathing in all the fake chemical fog.

8

It was Saturday night, and Candace was waiting in the alcove for the first people to come through the maze. "Are you as tired as I am?" she asked Reggie.

"I was until about twenty minutes ago. I think they pump caffeine into the fog."

Just thinking about the fog made Candace cough. She saw movement at the entrance.

"I think we're about to get our first visitors," she said.

Sure enough, several people were moving slowly down the hallway. Candace waited, having gotten really good at timing things just right, and then jumped out right in front of the first people who stopped suddenly.

She recognized her parents and smiled at them but ran through like she should, Reggie on her heels. During the finale she saw that they had managed to work their way to the back of the group, and they paused in front of her and Ray and snapped a picture before exiting the maze.

"My parents," Candace explained before running back to the start. *I just hope they don't give that picture to Tamara. Who knows what she'd do with it!*

Impossible as it seemed, there were even more people than the night before. Halfway through the night Candace was sure she was going to collapse from exhaustion, but somehow she made it through.

When she finally got home, she found a note on the kitchen table from her parents.

We had a great time! You were amazing. We'll talk in the morning. Love, Mom and Dad.

Candace smiled and took the note up to her room where she safely stowed it in her box of special keepsakes. She couldn't wait to talk to them in the morning.

The morning came, and Candace realized almost immediately that she wouldn't be talking to her parents. Her throat hurt terribly, and she quickly discovered she had lost her voice. The constant screaming for two nights had caught up to her.

When she went downstairs, she received enthusiastic praise from her parents while her mom made her some tea with lemon and honey for her throat.

"I haven't had that much fun in years!" her dad said. "They've really done something special with that Scare event."

"We made it to all the mazes and most of the haunted rides," her mom explained.

"And I know you're going to think we're biased, but your maze was definitely the best."

Candace smiled.

"And you were amazing," her mom chimed in.

Her dad pushed the picture he had taken of her across the table. "I printed it this morning. You look great, and I think I framed that picture pretty well, even if I do say so myself," he bragged.

She got up and gave him a quick hug.

"Now try not to say anything for the next two days so your voice can heal," her mom said, handing her the tea.

Candace drank it gratefully. It felt soothing to her raw throat. Her parents continued to tell her all about their adventures through the park until she was envious. She was going to have to find a way to work it so that she got a chance to go through some of the mazes herself. She figured as long as she steered clear of the Mummy's Curse, she couldn't get lost and so hopefully she wouldn't panic. That was the only maze that was a maze in the true sense of the word. The others had only one path and players could get out by continuing to move forward.

She spent the day doing some homework and resting. By the time she got to The Zone she could speak a little. Candy wasn't going to be screaming through the maze but at least she could still run. She was never really sure anyway how well the players could hear her screaming above the pounding music.

She got into position in her maze and found herself daydreaming about going home and getting some more sleep. At least she had made it this far. She could make it through the first weekend of Scare, and it should be all coasting downhill from there. Kurt had promised her that it would get easier.

The fog and music started up, the cue that players could only be about ten minutes behind. Candace braced herself for the onslaught.

The first group was a bunch of younger girls who screamed hysterically and clutched at each other when Candace jumped out in front of them. The sight brought her joy, and she fought the urge to laugh. Each time she jumped out in front of the group, they were more hysterical than the last.

Finally when Ray grabbed Candace, one of the girls at the back of the group screamed and bolted for the exit. The entire group of girls fell on the floor screaming and flailing about.

Candace just pretended to struggle harder while Ray cackled like a maniac. "I'll be coming for you next," he said, bending close to one of the girls. They screamed louder and scooted on all fours all the way to the exit.

"Oh, that was good," Ray laughed as he let Candace go. She nodded and gave him a huge smile before returning to the start.

As the night wore on she grew more tired, but she kept putting all she had into it. She mistimed one group when she did her initial run and nearly ran into the leader. She made it to the curtained-off section and moved quickly to her next position. She stared intently at the mirror, determined not to get a late jump again.

She saw a flash of something that seemed out of place. It looked like someone in costume, but not one of the psychos. She shook her head and got ready to make her next run. She saw the group move into position. She jumped out and ran. Suddenly a board gave way beneath her foot and the other end snapped up and hit her in the head. *Just like in the cartoons*, she thought dazedly.

She fell backward, and the players ran around her screaming. *They probably think that's supposed to happen.* Candace struggled to a sitting position. She needed an umpire.

"Help!" she tried to shout, but it came out as little more than a whisper. *No one will ever hear me.*

She managed to stand up and it made her dizzy. She coughed, choking on the fog, and moved along the maze, her left hand on the wall guiding and supporting her. It seemed like it took forever but she finally found an umpire.

"What happened?" the man in black asked, putting an arm around her.

"A board came loose, hit me in the head," she said pointing behind her.

He pulled his walkie-talkie off his belt. "This is Cameron in Candy Craze. There's been an accident. Don't let any more players in until we can check it out. There's a loose board that hit Candy in the head. I'm taking her to the nurse."

There was a bunch of return chatter, but Candace couldn't hear what they were saying. She leaned on Cameron, and he guided her to a part of the maze she hadn't been in and then through a back door into a building. From there they took an elevator down to a hallway under the park that Candace had never known was there. In five minutes they were back up at street level and at the nurse's.

"Thank you," Candace said. "I can take it from here."

She walked toward the back where they had the examination tables. She remembered it well from when she had been injured over the summer.

Candace came to an abrupt stop. There on one of the tables a mummy lay perfectly still. She stared for a moment. It looked so perfect she thought it might be a prop. Logic, however, told her that only a real person would be lying down on a table in the nurse's station.

Suddenly the mummy rose at the waist, and Candace jumped and let out a little shriek. She backed toward the door.

"Candace, is that you?" the mummy asked suddenly.

Candace stopped and stared for a moment. "Yes. Who are you?" she asked.

"It's Sue."

"Sue?" Candace asked, moving over to stand beside her. "That's you?"

"It's not the mummy," Sue said sarcastically.

Candace blushed. "Sorry, I'm just a bit jumpy."

"It's okay. What are you doing here?"

"I got hit in the head," Candace said.

"Ouch. You okay?"

"I'm hoping the nurse can tell me," Candace said. "Why are you here?"

"I got too hot, and apparently I fainted."

"Seriously?"

Sue nodded. It looked weird. Candace could see just her eyes and her mouth, but the rest of her face was tightly wrapped in the bandages.

"That makes me the second," Sue said. "At least I wasn't the first."

"Josh told me that mummies often fainted from the heat. I guess it's true," Candace said.

"Yeah, there is just no air. My skin can't breathe, and it gets so hot in the maze. I started to get dizzy. I tried to head for an exit, but I guess I didn't make it."

"Wow. At least I'm still conscious," Candace said.

"Nothing like a little perspective, huh?" Sue asked. Her laugh sounded weak, and she was slumping a little.

"Maybe you should lie back down," Candace suggested. "You want me to help you get some of your costume off?"

"I'll help her do that," the nurse said, bustling in. "The only thing I want you doing is finding your own cot," she said to Candace.

Candace nodded. Fortunately the one next to Sue was vacant, and she eased herself down onto it. She sat for a moment, not really wanting to lie down in the short skirt.

"If you don't want to lie down, at least sit still until I can take a look at you," the nurse said, noticing her discomfort.

"Thank you," Candace said. As soon as she sat, she realized just how tired she was. She watched as the nurse unwound the bandages from Sue's head and Sue's face appeared bit by bit.

At last Sue's head was completely free, and she sighed in relief. Her face was really pale. The nurse got her some water, and then Sue drank it and lay back down.

"Are you doing this on top of the janitorial job?" Candace asked.

"Yes."

"Why?"

"Extra money," Sue said.

"Isn't it really hard to do both with your college classes?" Candace asked.

"You have no idea," Sue said, sounding like she might cry.

"What's wrong?" Candace asked.

"Nothing. I still don't feel well," Sue said.

Candace got the distinct impression that there was something Sue wasn't telling her. Before she could press her, though, the nurse bustled over.

"Okay, missy, it's your turn. What happened to you?"

"I got hit in the head," Candace explained.

The nurse pulled a small flashlight out of one of her smock pockets and shined it in Candace's eyes.

"Where did you get hit?" she asked.

Candace pointed, and the nurse pulled apart her hair and examined the skin. It still hurt, and Candace could tell there was a slight bump. The nurse made tsking sounds as she looked it over.

"How bad is she?" Sue asked.

"Well, she has a mild concussion. Doesn't look like anything to write home about. However, no sleeping for you for at least eight hours," the nurse said, directing the last at Candace.

"But all I want is to go home and go to bed," Candace protested.

"I'm sorry, but you can't run that risk with a concussion. If you go to sleep and your brain swells too much, you might slip into a coma and never wake up."

"That would be bad," Candace said.

"Very bad," the nurse agreed.

"How on earth am I going to stay awake that long?" she croaked. "I'm already exhausted."

"You'll have to get someone to stay up with you."

"Who?"

"I think I can help there," Josh said, appearing as if by magic.

"My hero," Candace said. She stared at his fangs and cape. "Is it wrong to call a vampire my hero?" she asked.

"Wow, you're really out of it," he said. "Do you want me to take you home or to a hospital?"

"Home," she said.

He looked at the nurse, who nodded. "That should be fine as long as you keep her awake until morning."

"I think I can handle that," he said. "Come on, let me take you home."

She was grateful Josh was there. With how tired she was and how much her head hurt, she wasn't up to figuring out how to get there by herself. She was definitely getting a little more fuzzy-headed.

9

"Thanks for bringing me home, Josh," Candace said as she climbed the steps to her door.

"That's what friends do."

"You don't have to stay and keep me up all night."

"I beg to differ. I promised the nurse I would."

"Thank you. I appreciate it."

She unlocked the door, and they went inside. All she wanted to do was sleep, but she knew that she couldn't.

"I better let my parents know what happened," she said.

"That would probably be a good idea. I wouldn't want your dad to be surprised in the morning when he sees me on the couch."

Candace nodded. Her head was still throbbing, and she wished she didn't have to wait a couple more hours before taking more aspirin. She climbed the stairs and knocked lightly on her parents' door.

She heard rustling inside, and then her father said, "Come in."

She opened the door and moved inside, leaving it open so the light from the hallway lit her way. Her mom sat up and switched on the lamp next to the bed. She yawned and glanced at the clock. "Aren't you home early?"

"Yeah. I got hit in the head by a loose board. The nurse at The Zone said I have a mild concussion, nothing bad."

"What happened?" her dad asked.

Candace told them briefly. Her mom started to get up. "Well, I better make you some cocoa. You can't go to sleep with a concussion."

"It's okay," Candace said. "Josh brought me home. He's downstairs, and he's volunteered to stay up with me."

Her parents exchanged a quick glance. Candace wasn't sure what it meant, but she didn't feel like speculating. "It's okay, we'll be downstairs."

"It's Josh?" her dad asked.

"Yes."

"That's fine," her mom said. "Josh is a very nice young man." She reached for her robe.

"I said you don't have to stay up," Candace said. "I don't want you to have to miss work in the morning."

"I won't be up long. I'll just make you and Josh some cocoa."

"Thanks," Candace said. Cocoa sounded good, and she was too tired to argue. She followed her mom downstairs.

"Good evening, Josh," she said.

"Good evening Mrs. Thompson," Josh said, rising from the couch. "I'm sorry to disturb you like this."

"Nonsense. I'm just grateful you brought Candace home and have volunteered to keep her up all night."

"It was no trouble."

"Have you had a chance to call your parents yet?"

"I called them and let them know where I was going to be while I waited for the nurse to release Candace."

"Good. Come into the kitchen. I'll make us all some cocoa."

They sipped hot cocoa and talked for half an hour before Candace's mom excused herself. "You're sure you don't need me?" she asked one last time as she started up the stairs.

"No, we'll be fine," Candace said, moving with Josh into the living room and sinking wearily onto the couch.

Josh sat beside her, and she looked at him for a minute. "What shall we talk about?" she asked.

"I heard from my brother, James, this morning," he said.

"I didn't know you had a brother. Where is he?"

"Iraq."

Candace felt suddenly much more awake. "Is he okay?"

Josh nodded. "He's due to get out in a few weeks. It looks like he's going to make it home just in time for Christmas."

"That's wonderful!" Candace said.

"Yeah, we're all pretty excited. Mom and Dad are already planning a big coming-home party for him."

"So he must be a few years older."

"He's five years older. He breezed through college in just under three years and immediately signed up to serve two years."

"Wow!"

"Yeah. He's an overachiever. Kinda runs in the family."

Candace smiled. "So, what's he going to do now?"

"Looks like he's going to work with Dad."

"How about you? What are your plans?"

"Long-term or short-term?" he asked.

"For college."

"I'm pretty sure I'm going to go to Florida Coast."

"What are you going to major in?"

"That I haven't decided yet. I'm thinking of going in as un-declared. I want to sample a little bit of everything before I make a decision."

"No family business for you?"

He shrugged. "Maybe. How about you? Where are you looking at going?"

"I was thinking I'd apply to Cal State."

"Planning on staying at home?"

She nodded.

"That's cool. And your major? What do you want to be when you grow up?"

"Grown up."

"Smart aleck."

She smiled. "Seriously? I haven't a clue. I mean, not at all."

"I think you'd be a terrific Game Master."

"Please."

"No, seriously. I still think your Balloon Races is an awesome idea."

"And I think you're the one with the concussion."

"Yeah, that's it. You should think about it though. You don't know what you want to do anyway."

"Okay. I'll think about it if we can change the subject," she said. "I have a concussion, I want to be amused. This is too much heavy thinking."

"Deal. Now, how can I entertain you?"

"Tell me another secret," she said.

"Sorry. You already know the only one I have. Careful, though, or I'll make you tell me another one."

Candace was sitting in the nurse's office at The Zone on Tuesday afternoon, having just finished her follow-up for the concussion. She was staring at Martha, her supervisor from the summer, who was filling out some forms the nurse had handed her after examining Candace. Martha was a wise older woman with lively eyes and a gravelly voice. She had stuck by Candace through the hard times over the summer, and Candace had been relieved to see her in the nurse's office until Martha had delivered the news.

"Why am I being taken out of the maze?" Candace asked indignantly. "I didn't do anything wrong. It wasn't my fault the board was loose."

"I know that, Candace," Martha said with a heavy sigh. "It's policy, though, that if someone gets seriously injured, they are moved to a different position for four weeks until a full investigation has been done and the nurse clears the injured person to return to her previous duties."

"But, this is Scare. Four weeks and the whole thing will be over with."

"I know."

"So that's it. I'm not going to be working Scare at all?"

"I didn't say that. We do have a position we'd like to move you to."

"What?" Candace asked.

"We need a candy corn vendor."

"You have got to be kidding me."

"Wish I was," Martha said with a sigh.

"I'm going to be back on cart detail?"

"Yes."

"Don't I have any other options?"

"Not unless you want to quit. I wouldn't blame you by the way."

Candace was stunned. After everything that had happened, she was going to end up as a cart vendor again. She briefly thought about quitting, but she had committed to working Scare and she wanted to do that.

"Okay. Tell me when and where," Candace said with a sigh.

"You'll only work Scare nights. Same hours as before. You can pick up your cart in the cart storage area before the park opens. You can start Thursday."

On Wednesday Candace waited in the office for her appointment with the guidance counselor, Mr. Anderson. She was glad to have a distraction from the drama that was The Zone. She wasn't looking forward to returning to cart duty the next night.

She glanced down at the paper in her hand. She had with her a list of questions she wanted to ask Mr. Anderson about colleges and majors. She was a little nervous, but mostly excited. Going to college was going to be cool, something new and exciting. She was looking forward to it, even though she still didn't know where she wanted to go or what she wanted to do once she got there.

"Miss Thompson, you can go in now," the secretary said.

Candace stood and crossed to Mr. Anderson's office door. She opened it, carefully closed it all the way behind her, and then sat down across the desk from him. Mr. Anderson was a stern-looking man in his fifties with dark hair that was gray at the sides. Candace had seen him around campus frequently, but this was the first opportunity they'd had to formally meet.

"Candace Thompson?" he asked, shuffling a folder to the top of the stack in front of him.

"Yes," she said. "Pleased to meet you," she added for good measure.

He smiled briefly. "And you. I am, of course, Mr. Anderson, the guidance counselor."

He flipped open the folder, looked at the paper on top, and then leaned back in his chair and regarded her with a level gaze. "So, tell me, Candace. What do you see for your future?"

It was a pretty open-ended question, especially since that was the question she was most in need of help answering. She took a deep breath. "I still haven't decided what career I'm interested in pursuing, but I'm hoping I can figure that out by the end of my first year of college."

"So, is there a particular major you wanted to declare, or were you thinking of applying as undeclared?"

"Undeclared," she said.

"And is there a particular college you had in mind?"

"I was thinking of Cal State, but I also wanted to explore my other options."

"I see," he said, glancing down at the folder again. "Have you considered community college as a possibility? Many students like to go to get their feet wet and get some of their electives out of the way."

"I don't want to go to community college. I'm definitely going for my bachelor's degree, and I don't want to change schools partway through," she said.

"I've been glancing over your school file in preparation for this meeting. Are there any extracurricular activities that you're involved with? Sports, Girl Scouts, youth orchestras, anything like that?"

"Nothing like that. I had a summer job as a cotton candy vendor at The Zone, and I'm working the Scare event."

He jotted something down in the file.

"Why do you want to go to college?" he asked.

"To get my degree so that I can start on a career," she said. She wondered why he was asking. College was a no-brainer in her book.

"Candace, I'm going to be frank with you."

She wasn't sure she liked the sound of that or the look he was giving her.

"Yes?"

"I can tell you haven't been applying yourself to anything."

"What do you mean?" she asked.

"The last three years you've gotten mostly *B*s with a few *A*s. The teacher comments indicate that you didn't struggle for the *B*s. They came fairly easy to you, and with only a little effort you could have had a four point oh. Couple that with the fact that you have participated in no extracurricular activities, no community service, or probably anything more remarkable than going to the mall, and I come up with a picture of you that tells me one thing: You don't try very hard. Given that, I'm wondering what you think college is going to be like. You're not going to be able to coast your way through that too. You're going to have to really work, and unfortunately there's nothing in your record that indicates to me or to a prospective college that you have the discipline or ambition to succeed."

"But I am disciplined. I held a job all summer."

"Unfortunately that isn't compelling proof that further education is the right option for you. Maybe you would be better off just entering the workforce directly out of high school."

"No! I refuse to do that. I'm not going to spend my life working as a cotton candy vendor or something like that. Just because I don't know what I want to be doesn't mean that I don't know what I want out of life. I want to have a career. I want to have an education. I want to have a family and enough money that I don't have to stress each month about paying bills. I'm not likely to get any of those things without going to college."

"There's the fire! Unfortunately, it seems like it only comes out when you're provoked."

She stared at him. She was angry, and she was hurt. Worse than that, though, was a creeping sense of humiliation. Deep down she was afraid that he was right. The first thing she had ever really worked at or fought for was her job at The Zone. So, while she wanted to throw everything he had said back in his face, she couldn't.

"I don't know what to say," she said finally.

"At least that's the truth," he said. "Look. I'd like you to prove me wrong. Go home, take a couple of weeks, and think about what I said. Come back next month and we'll talk about your options. You don't have to apply to every school tomorrow."

She stood stiffly, willing herself not to cry. The irony was not lost on her that she had been in Mr. Anderson's shoes over the summer when nagging Kurt about his future. If it weren't for her pushing him, he wouldn't be attending community college. Now someone was telling her that she had no ambition and didn't try. She realized how humiliated Kurt must have felt, and she felt sorry for that.

She left Mr. Anderson's office, retrieved her things from her locker, and walked out to the parking lot. She sat down on a bench to wait for Tamara to get out of class. So far this was shaping up to be a rotten week. She had been looking forward to discussing colleges with Mr. Anderson, and the whole thing had seemed like some cruel joke.

Was Mr. Anderson right? Had she spent her life just coasting? She didn't want to think so, but she couldn't actually find proof to the contrary. By the time Tamara came out to the parking lot, Candace had worked herself into a state of sheer misery.

"Ouch!" Tamara said when she saw her. "That bad?"

Candace nodded, not trusting herself to speak just yet.

Twenty minutes later Candace had told Tamara everything around sips of a double hot chocolate with raspberry at their favorite coffee shop.

"He actually said that?" Tamara asked.

"Yes."

"Oh, man, what's he going to say to me?"

"I don't know."

"I was nervous enough already, but now I don't know how I'm going to go in there," Tamara admitted.

Candace just stared at her. "You'll be great. You always are. Dazzle him by just being you."

"You know, sometimes I think you have too high an opinion of me."

"It's only fair. It helps balance my low opinion of myself."

"Come on, Candace, don't say that. Shake it off. The guy's a jerk. He doesn't know you."

"It sure seemed like he did," she said, taking another swig of the steaming chocolate brew.

"Well, he doesn't. The Candace I know is smart and strong and can do anything she sets her mind to."

"Yeah, but how often have you seen me set my mind to something?" Candace asked.

"All summer."

"Besides working at The Zone over the summer."

Tamara was quiet for a minute, clearly trying to think of something to say.

"See? That's just the problem. I can't think of anything either," Candace sighed.

"Well, then let's stop thinking of the past and look to the future. What can you set your mind to tomorrow?"

It was a good question.

"I don't know."

"Then, I think you better spend some time trying to figure that out."

10

Thursday night arrived and Candace showed up at The Zone. She had swung by earlier to pick up her new uniform, which looked a lot like her old uniform except it was orange and black striped instead of pink and white. She waved at friends as she walked toward the cart storage area. Martha was there with a clipboard.

"I'm sorry, Candace," she said again.

"It's okay," Candace muttered. It was a lie. It wasn't okay with her at all, but what good would it have done to say that? No use in both of them starting the evening off miserable.

"You'll be selling packets of candy corn," Martha said. "They're two dollars each."

Candace nodded. At least it wasn't cotton candy. She wasn't sure if she could have taken that.

"You'll be on cart five," Martha said, gesturing to it.

The same cart she had had all summer. There was something particularly fitting about that. Candace walked up to the cart and eyed it suspiciously. "Hello, old friend."

As if in response, the cart whirred suddenly to life. The food carts at The Zone were totally automated. They could move themselves from location to location around the park as demand dictated. They could also be fitted to carry whatever was needed. A digital display sprang to life and the words *I missed you, Candy!* suddenly appeared.

Candace jumped. "Okay, now that's extra creepy," she muttered. For one horrible moment she thought the cart was talking to her. Then her brain settled on the more logical conclusion, someone was trying to be funny.

The cart headed off, and Candace walked beside it. When they arrived in the Splash Zone, the cart parked itself in a conspicuous place several yards from the exit to the Haunted Village maze. Candace looked around. She hadn't been to this part of the park since it got its Halloween theming.

During the summer the Splash Zone was one of the most popular areas of the park. The entire area was themed to look like a seaside fishing village. A river ran completely around the perimeter of the zone, and two footbridges allowed passage over the river to the zones on either side. The river fed the area's many water attractions, which included a log ride, a river-rafting ride, a water maze, a wave pool, and Kowabunga—a giant water slide. In the center of the zone, an island sat in a small lake. The island held a row of buildings that included shops, counter-service eateries, and a lighthouse with a restaurant at the top.

During the fall, fewer players ventured into the Splash Zone. The row of shops had been temporarily gutted and turned into the Haunted Village maze. The whole zone was filled with fake fog, and the light from the lighthouse cut an eerie swathe through it, bathing everything it touched in a freakish glow. The cry of a foghorn boomed out periodically, and the lapping water sounded more ominous than it had during the summer.

Candace shivered. The place was definitely competing to be the creepiest in the park, and in her estimation it won, hands down. It actually felt like a real place that had been abandoned by time and left to decay. It wasn't hard to imagine that such a place could be haunted.

A grizzled-looking fisherman with a hook for a hand walked by, tipping his hat to her. He seemed to disappear into the fog as he walked toward the buildings.

"Extra creepy," she said out loud, eager to hear the sound of anyone's voice, even just her own.

As the minutes ticked by and no one else appeared, she started to feel even more unnerved. Finally she heard voices and then saw a group of costumed characters moving toward her. They had a variety of props between them, including fishing nets, lanterns, and chains. Some of them waved at her before they headed into the maze. She relaxed slightly. Umpires followed close on their heels, and the Game Master showed up last.

A minute later the soundtrack for the maze started up. Instead of pounding rock music, this maze had creaking chains and ghostly howls punctuated by occasional bloodcurdling screams and the cries of seabirds.

It was interesting to see the contrast between the two mazes. This maze was going for a sense of anticipation, relying on sudden sound and movement to finish what overactive imaginations started. The Candy Craze maze was going for confusion and heart-pumping adrenaline. The looks and sounds of both mazes were geared toward those goals. Players were expected to walk slowly, hesitantly forward in the Haunted Village, afraid of what might lurk around every corner. Players in the Candy Craze, on the other hand, were expected to run, terrified of what might catch them.

Ten minutes later the first players arrived. They had been inside the maze only a few seconds when the screaming began. Candace couldn't help but smile. At the end of the day, that was what Scare was all about.

The second group of people out of the maze made a beeline for her cart. For the rest of the evening she discovered just how in demand candy corn was. She had suspected that it would be popular, but she'd had no idea how many people would come looking for the distinctly Halloween sugar rush.

As she served up bag after bag, she enjoyed listening to them talking about where they were going, the scariest things they had seen so far, and what they were thinking about their experience. The more she listened, the more curious she became. She really was going to have to find a way to get enough time off so that she could check out all the mazes.

She found she was actually enjoying herself. Then, about halfway through her shift, she heard something that gave her pause.

"I was here last weekend, and that's definitely a different girl in the Candy Craze maze. She's so much better than the one from last weekend."

Candace flushed, realizing that he was talking about her and her replacement. She never heard who was going to be playing Candy in the maze since her unfortunate departure.

"Yeah, the girl tonight was totally believable … and hot," another guy said.

Better … believable … Candace didn't like the sound of either of those. She nearly miscounted the change that she gave back to the next customer in line. *Get a grip!* she told herself. They probably brought in some seasoned pro who'd been working Scare for years. Maybe she was even a professional actress. It seemed unlikely, but it at least made Candace feel better.

Martha showed up to give her a quick break and to check up on her. Candace decided to make a beeline for Candy Craze to see for herself who the girl who had replaced her was. The person controlling the line recognized her and waved her into the maze at the end of a group.

It was strange to be walking through the maze, observing it as a player. Being at the back of the line she didn't get a good look at the girl playing Candy. She could, however, hear her whimpering and begging for her life instead of screaming.

That's lame. She's making Candy seem like too much of a wimp, she thought. Each time Candy appeared, she seemed more pathetic than the last, sobbing louder each time.

Finally the finale arrived, and the first thing Candace noticed was that the girl wasn't struggling in her captor's arms to try and free herself, she was hanging limp like a rag doll, defeated and pathetic. The second thing she noticed was the girl's face.

It was Lisa.

The players ran to the exit, but Candace stood staring at Lisa who finally saw her and smiled smugly. *Lisa! How could they pick Lisa!*

Lisa was Kurt's ex-girlfriend. She had made Candace's life miserable over the summer and even lied to try to get her fired. Candace was furious. Of all people to be replaced by, why did it have to be her?

She made it back to the cart, and Martha took one look at her face and said, "Lisa was the only one they could move there in time."

"There had to be another choice," Candace said.

"I'm sorry," Martha answered. The older woman then beat a hasty retreat.

The fact that Martha knew somehow made it even worse. It was like a betrayal. As she handed out bag after bag of candy corn, Candace wondered how she could get Lisa out of the maze.

Fifteen minutes later, as luck would have it, Candace spotted Tish walking toward the Haunted Village maze.

"Tish!" Candace called.

Tish looked at her as though she had no idea who she was. "Tish, it's me, Candy," Candace said, swallowing her pride and using the nickname.

"Oh, Candy, what are you doing there?" Tish asked, walking over.

"I got injured in the maze last weekend, and policy said that I had to be taken out for a while," Candace explained.

"I heard something about that," Tish said. "I'm glad you're okay. The irony is wonderful though. You survive the real thing only to be injured in the re-creation."

Candace gritted her teeth. She thought about trying to explain, again, that there had never been a psycho killer. She doubted Tish would listen, and Candace had a more pressing concern. "Yeah. Anyway, the girl that's playing … me … in the maze right now … her name is Lisa, and she's playing … me … really wimpy. It's embarrassing. Could you please have her removed?"

"Sorry. She's getting good buzz, and the lines are longer than ever."

"But, it's not right! I mean, that's not who I am."

"Are you sure?"

"Of course I'm sure! I was the one trapped in the park with the killer, I oughta know how it was!" Candace came to an abrupt stop, horrified. *I'm buying into my own urban legend!* "That's not what I wanted to say," she began, but Tish cut her off.

"Sorry. Wish I could help. Enjoy Scare." Tish moved away, leaving Candace standing there feeling like an idiot.

Candace couldn't believe how Tish had just blown her off. *Last weekend she thought I was the best thing ever. Wow, is she fickle.*

It wasn't right. If Candace was the Game Master in charge of a maze, she would certainly care about authenticity. And if the maze was loosely based on a real person, she would most certainly want that person's input and want to keep her happy.

Her thoughts were interrupted by a seriously shrill scream from the maze followed by someone shouting. Candace turned her eyes toward the maze. She'd been outside of the maze for nearly four hours and hadn't heard anything like that before. Something felt wrong.

A minute later security showed up on the scene, and she got a sick feeling in the pit of her stomach. Ten minutes later they had sealed off the area, set up a barricade, and escorted players out of the Splash Zone.

A security officer hurried by Candace, and she hailed him. "What's going on?" she asked.

"Somebody attacked one of the girls working in the maze," he said before moving on.

Candace sat down on the ground, heart racing. She had known something was wrong. She watched the referees coming out of the maze and being questioned one by one by security. Paramedics arrived with a stretcher, and she could see them put a girl on it. They carried her right past Candace on their way out, and she saw with horror that there was blood oozing through the bandages covering her chest. Her eyes were open, and she looked terrified.

Candace closed her eyes and prayed for the girl, the paramedics, the referees who had been inside, and the players. She also prayed that security would find whoever had done it quickly so they could all rest easy.

Finally a security officer approached her. "You were out here when it happened, right?"

"Yes."

"Did you see or hear anything?"

"I heard a really loud scream and then some shouting. It sounded like there was something wrong. That was all though. What happened?"

"Apparently, some guy slashed Vicki, one of the referees, across the chest with a hook. Unfortunately, the only referee with a hook is that guy sitting over there," he said pointing. "And his hook is made of rubber."

Candace looked and saw the guy in question. He was dressed like a naval captain.

"What about the fisherman?" Candace asked.

"What fisherman?"

"I saw a fisherman go into the maze before the others. He had a hook on his hand."

"We haven't seen anyone like that." He spoke into his walkie-talkie. "Sweep the maze again, check every corner. We're looking for a fisherman with a hook hand."

It was so surreal that Candace wanted to laugh, but she remembered the frightened eyes of the girl as they carried her past, and she couldn't laugh. Something awful had happened.

"Would you recognize him if you saw him?"

"I might," Candace said. "I mean, I would certainly recognize his clothes, and I might recognize him."

"Tell you what, show me where you were standing and how far away he was from you."

Candace showed him.

"I'm going to have everyone walk by, and you tell me if any of them looks familiar."

"Okay."

Five minutes later the last referee walked past Candace's cart. She shook her head in frustration. None of them were dressed as the fisherman had been. Worse, she was pretty sure none of the people she saw could have been him.

She spent another half hour answering questions before she was finally released for the evening. She used the intercom on the cart to report in, and a signal was sent to the cart to bring it back to base.

As she turned in the cart, she gave Martha a weak smile. It wasn't her fault Candace had gotten hurt. Besides, worrying about Lisa in the Candy Craze maze seemed petty in comparison to what had just happened in the other maze.

"You okay, sweetie?"

Candace nodded. "If they catch the guy, could you let me know? I'd sleep better."

"We all would," Martha said with a sigh. "There's no way to keep a lid on this thing. Management's trying to decide if they want to shut down the park early tonight. I'm hoping they don't. It'll cause a panic, and that's one thing we don't need on our hands."

"I'll see you tomorrow," Candace said.

Once in her car, she checked the backseat and made sure all her doors were locked. Then she stopped and prayed again. She didn't like to think that such things happened in the world, even though she knew they did. It was just hard to confront them, though, especially at her place of work.

11

Josh called her in the morning, waking her out of a sound slumber. "What is it?" she asked sleepily.

"They're pretty sure they know who the guy was who hurt Vicki."

"Did they catch him?" she asked, sitting up straight.

"Not yet. It turns out that Vicki just broke up with her boyfriend, a real piece of work."

"Eeww. That's almost worse than it just being some psycho," Candace said.

"Yeah, but the police are looking for him, and it looks like we won't have a rogue slasher on our hands."

"That is good news. Is she going to be okay?"

"Yeah, she got lucky. She was wearing several layers of clothing, and it turned out to be more of a scratch. Only needed a few stitches from what I hear."

"That's a relief," Candace said. *Thank you, God!*

"Yeah. I heard about Lisa playing you by the way. Sorry."

"Don't worry about it. Last night's incident gave me some perspective."

"Gotcha. Well, have a good day at school, and I'll see you tonight."

"Okay," she said, closing her cell. She glanced at the clock. The alarm would be going off in about fifteen minutes. She briefly contemplated trying to fall back asleep but visions of hitting the snooze alarm until noon filled her head. With a sigh she turned off the alarm and got up.

By the time the school day was over, she was wishing she had stayed in bed. Four of her teachers had just assigned papers all to be due in about two weeks. By the time she made it home, she was feeling more than a little overwhelmed.

She walked in the door and upstairs to her bedroom where she decided the only way she was going to make it through the weekend was if she took a nap right there and then. Two hours later when she awoke, she felt much better and ready to tackle just about anything.

In the Locker Room at work she was stowing her stuff when Josh stalked in wearing his full vampire costume. "Please," he said, trying to sound like Dracula, "I am looking for a quick bite."

"Look somewhere else!" she laughed.

"These modern women, they do not understand Dracula," he moaned.

She rolled her eyes at him. He chose a locker and started stashing his street clothes. Candace walked over to the bulletin board to see if there were any notices she needed to be aware of.

An announcement on the board caught her eye. *Needed! Volunteers to help organize Sugar Shock event. See Martha.*

"Hey, Josh."

"Yeah?"

"What's Sugar Shock?" Candace asked, pointing toward the flyer.

"Sugar Shock is the event for all the younger kids during the day on Halloween. There's trick-or-treating and costume contests, and Freddie McFly and Mr. Nine Lives do a show."

"That's so cool," she said. "I wish I'd known about that when I was young enough to go."

"It is cool," Josh agreed.

"So, why do they need volunteers for it?" she asked.

"Because it's on Halloween. Most people are gearing up for the biggest night of Scare and are getting as much rest as they possibly can. No one wants to help run Sugar Shock, because they'll be worn out by the time Scare starts."

"But somebody has to run it," Candace said.

"Yeah. The supervisors usually draw straws, and this year it looks like Martha got the short one. They usually spend most of their time trying to bully, bribe, or beg people to do stuff for Sugar Shock."

For some reason that just seemed sad to Candace. She thought the whole event sounded cool, and she bet it was fun to see all the kids in their costumes. Every Halloween since she had stopped trick-or-treating, she had been the one to answer the door and pass out candy.

"You thinking of volunteering?" Josh asked.

"Yes."

"Good for you! I know Martha would be relieved to have the help."

Candace nodded. She headed for the cart storage area to pick up her cart, hoping to find Martha running things over there. She was in luck. Martha looked like it had already been a rough time, and Scare hadn't even started for the evening.

"Hey, Candace. Cart five's all ready for you. You're a few minutes early though."

"I was hoping to talk to you for a second."

"Shoot," the older woman said.

"I wanted to help with Sugar Shock."

"Ha ha. Very funny. Did Gib put you up to this?"

"No," Candace said, surprised at Martha's reaction. "I saw the flyer and I want to help."

Martha stared at her hard for a moment, and then a glimmer of what looked like relief showed in her eyes. "Really?" she asked.

"Yes."

"You know it's during the day on Halloween, right?"

"Yes."

"And you'll still work Scare?"

"Yes."

"If you do this, there's no changing your mind. No 'I'm sorry, Martha, I just can't handle it.' No backing out or calling in sick or quitting."

"No, of course not," Candace said. Martha was starting to scare her.

"Bless you!" Martha cried, suddenly throwing her arms around Candace.

"Okay, Martha, now you're really scaring me," Candace said.

The older woman pulled away and wiped her eyes on the back of her hands. "You have no idea how hard it is to get help running that event," she said.

"I don't get what the big deal is," Candace admitted.

"It's probably better that way," Martha said.

Candace was about to ask her what she meant by that when Martha's radio squawked to life. "Thank you," Martha said before reaching for it.

Candace nodded and moved toward cart five. This was her second night back on the cart, and in many ways it was like she had never left. Martha's reaction made Candace wonder if volunteering had been a bad idea, especially given all the homework her teachers were assigning. It would probably look really good on her college applications though. Also, she felt bad that no one wanted to help with the kids' event. It seemed like it would be fun.

The cart headed for the History Zone, which was just fine by Candace. She was hoping she'd get a chance to talk to Kurt. The next few weeks were going to be hectic, and there wasn't going to be much chance to see each other.

The cart parked outside the castle. Josh waved to her a few minutes later when he walked inside. Finally Candace saw several umpires head into the area, and she waved to Kurt. He broke off from the group and jogged over.

"Kiss break," he declared before kissing her.

"I like kiss break," she said. "I think I need more of them."

"Tell me about it," he said. "Things are getting crazy. I have a ton of homework for school."

"Me too. I was hoping, though, we could do something early next week."

"Unless you want to meet me on campus for dinner, I'm not sure when or how," he said.

"I could meet you on campus."

"You'd do that?" he asked.

"Of course. Just tell me when and where."

"Cool. Tuesday at five?"

"Works for me."

"Great, I'll text you and tell you where to meet me," he said.

"Hey, Kurt, hurry up!" one of the other guys shouted.

"That's my cue," Kurt said, giving her another quick kiss before running off.

🍁

Tuesday at five, Candace checked the text Kurt had sent her cell just to make sure she was in the right place. She was on the bench facing the main doors of Davis Hall, and it didn't seem like there could be any mistaking the location. The campus was a little rundown, and the buildings were cramped together, but there were some lovely green lawn areas and old trees that offered shade.

The doors to Davis Hall opened, and people came streaming out. They ranged in age from sixteen to sixty from the looks of it. She spotted Kurt as he made his way for her.

"Hi!" Kurt said, as she stood up. "Let's go get some food."

"Sounds good."

She fell into step beside him.

"How was class?"

"Brutal. It's hard to pay attention to the lecturer. He speaks really softly and laughs at jokes only he gets."

"At least he laughs," Candace said, thinking about her monotone history professor.

"I've got to write a paper for his class, and I have no idea how I'm going to pull that off."

"How long does it have to be?" Candace asked.

"Five pages."

That didn't sound too bad. "What's it on?" she asked.

"The American Revolution."

"What about it?"

"Anything about it."

"Well, that shouldn't be too bad. You know all kinds of stuff about that time period," she said, still not sure why he thought the assignment was going to be hard.

"It's awful. How am I supposed to figure out what to write about? I mean, they write books on the topic. How am I supposed to write something meaningful in five pages?"

"Maybe it doesn't have to be meaningful," Candace suggested. "Or maybe you could just pick one thing to write about like a specific battle or one person. You could write about Benjamin Franklin. Of course, I'm not sure that you could use an interview with him in the History Zone as a resource," she joked.

"It's not funny," Kurt said, sounding grumpy.

"Sorry," Candace said. "I was just trying to cheer you up."

"You want to cheer me up? Say you'll write the paper for me."

"Now who's joking?" Candace asked with a laugh.

Kurt didn't smile. He couldn't possibly be serious, could he?

"So, where are we eating?" she asked quickly.

"Campus cafeteria."

"That should be fun."

"Wow! If you think that's fun, you need to get out more often."

"It will be fun," Candace protested. "We're together. And besides, who knows if we'll have any time for dates until November."

He put his arm around her shoulders, and it made her feel good. They were almost to the cafeteria when Candace spotted a familiar figure.

"Hey, Sue!"

"Oh, hi!" the other girl said, looking startled.

"What are you doing here?"

"I'm going to school here," Sue said.

That seemed odd. Over the summer Sue had said she was getting ready to start Cal State.

"So, not Cal State then?" Candace asked.

Sue shook her head. "This is cheaper. Plus I can get my prerequisites out of the way."

"Oh. So, how are things?"

"Busy," Sue admitted. "I'm running to class."

"And we're running to the cafeteria," Kurt said, grabbing Candace's hand and tugging.

"Well, see you at The Zone," Candace said, as Kurt pulled her forward.

"Okay!" Sue called over her shoulder.

They made it into the cafeteria, which was large but crowded. Candace snagged a table while Kurt got the food. He returned a few minutes later with hamburgers and sodas.

"It's a good thing you're not a picky date," he quipped.

"I am picky. I picked you," she said, pleased with herself.

He smiled and reached for her hand. "That's why you're the best. So, what's going on with you?"

"Oh, school's been hectic. My drama class has been cool. The teacher mostly speaks in movie quotes."

"That's funny."

"It is, actually."

She smiled at him. She wanted to tell him about her meeting with Mr. Anderson, but she hesitated. She realized she was too embarrassed to repeat what he had said about her ... at least to Kurt. She had been the one to push Kurt to go to community college; she wasn't ready to admit that her guidance counselor had challenged her drive to attend college herself.

"So, are you liking college?" she asked instead.

He shrugged. "It's school. I've never been fond of school."

She looked down at her plate. "I'm sorry if I forced you to do something you didn't want to do," she said.

"You were just trying to look out for me," he said.

"Still, I'm sorry."

"Thanks, I appreciate that."

They ate the rest of the meal in silence. Everything Candace wanted to talk about—school, Lisa playing her in the maze, college—all seemed fraught with potential disaster. She was crazy about Kurt, but sometimes talking to him didn't go as well as she would hope. She guessed that, just like any relationship, it took time to work it all out.

When they had finished, she walked with him toward his next class. "I almost forgot," he said, breaking the silence, "my roommates and I are throwing a Halloween party the Wednesday before Halloween. That way it won't interfere with Scare stuff. Do you want to come?"

"I'd love to," she said, blushing. It would be their first official event they went to as a couple. "What should I wear?"

"It's a costume party, so come in costume."

"What costume are you going to wear?" she asked.

"I haven't decided yet."

She was on the verge of suggesting that they try and coordinate costumes when he glanced at his watch. "Gotta run," he said, pecking her on the cheek before disappearing into the building.

She sighed. As dates went it wasn't great, but it would have to do until the party.

When she got home her dad looked at her. "Everything okay?" he asked.

"Yeah. It's just hard juggling everything, you know? School, work, church, friends, boyfriend. How am I supposed to find time for everything?"

"You learn how to prioritize," he said. He looked at her more closely. "Is this really about you being too busy or did something upset you?"

"I wish I could spend more time with Kurt," she admitted.

"Ah, most girls wish for more time to spend with their boyfriends," he said with a smile.

She sat down on the couch. "Yeah, but it's weird. Even when we do spend time together it doesn't feel like quality time."

"How do you mean?"

"Tonight, I met him for dinner at the community college, and we ate in the cafeteria in between his classes."

"Sounds good so far."

"But all we really did was eat. We hardly talked at all."

"Is that normal for the two of you?"

"It seems so," she said. "I mean we talked a little more over the summer, but it was all the 'tell me about your family' and 'what's your favorite color?' stuff."

"And you wish you could talk about more with him?"

"Yes."

He cleared his throat, and she turned to look at him. "At the risk of being accused of not wanting you to date, may I make a suggestion?"

"Yes," she said, curiosity rushing through her.

"I think maybe Kurt isn't the guy for you."

She blinked several times. "What makes you say that?"

"You're obviously not fulfilled by the relationship. There's nothing really wrong, and yet you're not deliriously happy when you come home from a date with him."

He wasn't wrong, and there was no use trying to deny that. "What do I do?" she asked.

"As I see it, you have two choices. You can spend more time hoping that something magical happens between you, which is less likely the more time passes, or you can break up with him."

"I don't like the sound of either of those," she admitted.

"That's the problem with life. It rarely gives you neat decisions wrapped up in shiny paper with a bow on top. Most of the
important decisions in life are messy."

She nodded.

"Just, think about what I said."

"Okay, thanks, Daddy," she said.

"You're welcome."

She stood up and gave him a quick hug before heading up
to her room. It was too much to think about for the moment.
She knew she was acting like a coward, but she just needed
some more time to make up her mind.

12

The next day after school, Candace headed over to The Zone. Martha had left a message on her phone asking if they could meet and talk about Sugar Shock at four. Candace decided to take advantage of the hour she had to hunt for Becca. She found the other referee at her post in the Muffin Mansion.

"Long time no see," Candace said to Becca, giving her a quick hug.

"I know! I was beginning to think you had found another muffin supplier," Becca teased.

"Never!

"What can I get you?"

Candace looked at the vast display of muffins for a moment before making up her mind. The Muffin Mansion always had a huge variety of muffins available. In the spirit of Halloween, though, most of their muffins looked monstrous. Some were hideously deformed, others were gigantic, one type had nodules on either side that reminded Candace of the bolts on the neck of Frankenstein's monster. There were orange muffins, black muffins, and muffins with fake spiders on top.

"I'll try the pumpkin spice."

"A seasonal specialty," Becca said. "Excellent choice. Can I interest you in a specialty butter to go with it?"

"What is a specialty butter?" Candace asked.

"It's this new thing we're trying out. We unveiled it at the end of September," Becca explained. "We have created several specialty butters that can be paired quite nicely with certain muffins."

"And specialty butters are better than butter butter?"

"Absolutely. For example, I recommend pairing the pumpkin spice muffin with the cinnamon butter."

"Oh, that does sound good," Candace said.

"And it is."

"Okay, I'll give it a try."

Becca put her muffin in a bag along with a little container of butter and a plastic knife. "Can I get you anything else?" she asked.

"Some advice would be helpful," Candace admitted.

"Well, you're in luck. I just got off work like ten seconds ago."

"What do I owe?" Candace asked, reaching for her purse.

"It's on the house. I still don't eat my daily free muffin," Becca said.

"Sorry, I can't hook you up with sugar anymore," Candace said.

"It's not your fault. Let's go someplace we can talk."

They found a quiet bench in the park where they could talk undisturbed. Candace pulled her muffin out of the bag and started munching. "Wow! You're right, the cinnamon butter really makes this."

"Told you," Becca said, grinning. "I worked on that one myself."

Candace wondered briefly how she managed to do that without tasting anything with sugar in it. She decided to let it go. She had other things she wanted to talk about.

"So, what can I help with?" Becca asked.

"I guess I just needed someone to talk to. Life has been … frustrating lately."

"And so, naturally, I'm the first person you thought of," Becca joked.

Candace smiled. "Yes, actually. I consider you a friend, and I thought you could be more objective than Tamara or Kurt or even Josh."

"Okay, I've got my objective hat on," she said.

Candace took a deep breath.

"I feel stuck in a way. I have all these questions, and every time I try to get answers I only come up with more questions."

"Can you give me an example?"

Candace laughed bitterly. "I had a meeting with the school's guidance counselor. I was hoping he'd help me sort out what college I'm going to go to. Instead, he questioned that I should even be going to college. He told me I never applied myself at anything."

"Ouch."

"Then I had the accident in the maze, and suddenly I'm back to cart duty. It's like I keep taking gigantic steps backward."

"Did you ever consider that maybe you are where you are for a reason?" Becca asked.

"There's a reason for me being behind a cart?" Candace asked skeptically.

"Probably. Remind me some time to tell you how I came to work at the Muffin Mansion. It's a long, strange story. It taught me that everything has a purpose."

"Okay."

"So what else you got?"

"I'm stressing about Kurt. Things just don't look good down the road. I'm not sure how compatible his goals and mine are."

"I know what your problem is," Becca said.

"Really? Tell me."

"You're going through a fall time in your life."

"Excuse me?"

"Fall, like the season, like right now. Fall is the transition period between summer and winter. Summer is fun and carefree and cheery. Winter is also beautiful, but it's harder, not as carefree. You're no longer a child, and you're not really an adult yet. You're going through a transition, just like the seasons."

Candace thought about that for a minute. It made sense.

"What can I do about it?"

"Stop fighting it. You can't recapture your past anymore than you can speed up your future. Stop lamenting summer and stop trying to hurry winter. Just enjoy the fall."

"So, what should I do about Kurt?"

Becca gazed at her, smiling and benevolent. "Only you can choose how to truly live and enjoy the fall. Tell yourself what to do."

"I've spent so much time thinking about a possible future with Kurt that I've never spent time and effort on our present."

"And one thing is for certain, if you don't put forth any effort in the present, there is most certainly no future."

Candace shook her head. "What are you, the Yoda of The Zone?"

"I like to think of myself more as Captain Jack Sparrow."

"Yeah, but you make more sense," Candace laughed.

"Only sometimes," Becca said with a smile. "Just remember, crazy people often see the truth more clearly than sane ones."

"Thanks, Becca."

Candace glanced at her watch. "I've got a meeting with Martha. I should go."

"Have fun."

Martha had told Candace she would meet her in front of the castle. Candace left Becca and made her way to the History Zone. She arrived at the same time as Martha.

"I'm so glad you made it," Martha said, looking both happy and relieved.

"Wouldn't miss it," Candace said.

"Follow me," Martha said. She turned and walked down one side of the castle and then stopped.

"What is it?" Candace asked.

Martha pointed at the wall.

Puzzled, Candace took a closer look. Where Martha was pointing the bricks formed a particular pattern that looked almost like a door. Martha pressed her thumb against a brick next to the others and suddenly part of the wall opened inward.

Candace gasped in amazement. Martha stepped through, and Candace followed her. They were in a small room with a stairway on the right and an elevator on the left. Martha headed up the spiral stairs and Candace followed her.

When they reached the top, there was a massive wooden door barring the way. Once again Martha pressed her thumb to a brick next to the door and it too swung open.

Candace stepped inside. It was as if she had just entered a fairy tale. There were a dozen couches done in rich royal blue fabric with gold fleur-de-lis on them. Through an archway, Candace spotted a long table that probably could seat forty comfortably.

There were more openings to other rooms that became visible as she followed Martha deeper inside. Martha sat down on one of the couches and motioned for Candace to do the same. The couch was the most comfortable she had ever sat on, and she felt instantly at home.

"Welcome to one of the six Comfort Zones here in the park," Martha said.

"Wow! What are these places?" Candace asked.

"They're used mostly as corporate lounges. Sponsors and key employees are given access to them during their trips to the park. They also serve as meeting spaces for private events. And, occasionally, they serve other specialized purposes."

"And what purpose is this one serving?" Candace asked.

"This is command headquarters where we can plan out every last detail of Sugar Shock," Martha told her.

Candace felt her eyes bulge. "Here, seriously? We get to work in here?"

"Yes. On the way out, I'll key your thumbprint into the doors so that you can come up here without having to hunt me down. Once Sugar Shock is over, of course, we'll take your thumbprint out of the system. Go ahead, have a quick look around."

Candace stood up and quickly toured the rest of the Comfort Zone. There was a small room with a couple of cots in it. Another room held vending machines. There were also a couple of restrooms. She wondered briefly if Sue was responsible for cleaning them, or if there were other janitors who took care of the Comfort Zones.

Candace returned to the main room. "Where are the other Comfort Zones around the park?" she asked.

Martha shook her head. "We try to keep that quiet. I'm sure, however, that if you did some digging you could figure that out."

Candace nodded.

"Now, I don't have a lot of time right now, but I wanted to get you started thinking on a couple of things. We can meet again tomorrow night."

"Okay."

"We're going to need to recruit referees to work during Sugar Shock. Everyone works Halloween night, so working during the day on Halloween is strictly voluntary. Now, you're going to find that most people aren't going to want to volunteer. Be creative. Beg if you have to. We need at least seventy referees to pull this thing off."

"How many do we have now?" Candace asked.

"Two."

"Two?"

"Two," Martha affirmed.

"Two plus us?" Candace asked.

"Nope. Just us. You and I are it."

"Oh, my."

"Welcome to the Sugar Shock team," Martha said grimly.

They spent another ten minutes talking before Martha had to go. True to her word, though, she keyed Candace's thumbprint into the system. As they walked out the secret door in the castle, Candace felt a thrill. It had to be one of the best secrets in the world, or, at least, in The Zone.

Martha took off and Candace thought about leaving. Then she thought about her conversation with Becca and decided to try and hunt down Kurt first.

As it turned out, she found him in the Locker Room, having just come off his shift. "Hey, got a few minutes to talk?" she asked.

"Unfortunately, no."

"Oh."

"If you're heading toward the parking lot, though, I'll walk with you."

"Okay."

They left the Locker Room and headed for the parking lot.

"Is something wrong?" he asked.

"No, not really."

"Which is it? No, or not really?"

"It's just getting frustrating. It feels like we never see each other," Candace complained.

"Well, the good news is that will all change next year," Kurt said.

She cocked her head to the side. "How?" she asked.

"I figure you can attend community college with me. That way we can spend time on campus together. Eat at the cafeteria. Maybe we can even take some classes together," he said.

She stared at him for a moment without speaking. She had no intention of going to community college. He looked so enthusiastic, though, that she didn't know how to break the news to him. If it hadn't been for her nagging over the summer, he wouldn't be going to college at all.

She bit her lip. "Maybe," she said. She was a coward. Worse than that, she was a liar. She knew she should tell him the truth, but she didn't know how to do it without offending him. "Of course, pretty soon you can transfer to State," she said, hoping he would get the hint.

It turned out the hint was far too subtle. "After we get all our prerequisites out of the way, maybe," he said. "Then again, I'm thinking maybe just an associates degree will work for me. I'm not sure I need to go to all the trouble to get a BA."

And once again they were sailing into the dangerous territory called the future. Every time Candace compared her life goals with Kurt's, nothing ever seemed to match up. Sure, just a few days before she had told Josh she had no idea what she wanted to be, but she knew that a BA was the jumping off point to any kind of job she might want.

She thought about pressing Kurt further, asking him what he was thinking of getting a degree in. Maybe then she would have something to say. She still thought he would make a great history teacher, but she knew he couldn't do that without at least a BA and a credential.

"So, how's the umpiring going?" she asked.

"Good. Only a couple of incidents so far," he said.

"Like what?"

"A player hyperventilated in the maze, and it took awhile to calm her down enough to get her out of it. Another woman flailed her arms around and smacked her boyfriend in the face. She split his lip and there was some blood to clean up."

"Gross."

"Yeah. We had to shut the maze down for fifteen minutes while we dealt with that. Then, of course, there's the ghost."

"The ghost?" she asked, unsure which maze monster he was referencing.

"Yeah, the one that's haunting the theme park," he said.

"You don't seriously believe there's a ghost," she said.

"I do. Lots of weird stuff has happened this year, and it's the only thing that makes sense."

"A ghost makes sense?"

"Yeah. I mean, Sunday night one of the walls in the maze toppled over all by itself."

"I didn't hear about that," Candace said. He certainly hadn't mentioned it at dinner the night before.

"Yeah. Fortunately it happened five minutes before park opening. The crazy thing was the screws that were holding the wall in place were just missing. I had been in the maze for fifteen minutes before it happened, and I didn't see or hear a thing."

"Someone's just pulling a prank," Candace said.

"I don't think so."

Candace didn't believe in ghosts. It seemed, though, like Kurt did. One thing was for sure. There definitely was something going on at The Zone, and she'd bet anyone a month worth of pizzas that it wasn't supernatural.

13

Candace was really grateful to have Kurt as a boyfriend. It had nothing to do with looks, though he was gorgeous. It had nothing to do with his style, which was dashing. It had everything to do with his knowledge of esoteric history and his willingness to share it.

"Okay, so tell me again what happened to all the signers of the Declaration of Independence," she said, sitting across from him at the referee cantina.

He recounted the chilling list. Most of the men were killed or ruined outright. The sacrifice they had chosen to make was staggering. She scribbled furiously on her notepad as she listened. In her mind she imagined what their fates must have been like as destruction rained down on them, their homes, and families.

She asked him a dozen questions and took thorough notes. Fortunately her teacher was allowing interviews as a legitimate form of research for the paper.

"Thank you," she said at last, when he had answered every question on her list. "I think I have enough to write ten papers."

"No problem," he said, finishing up his dinner. "I'm back to work. You?"

"I'm going home to beat a paper on Colonial America out of this," she said, waving the notepad in the air.

"Good luck with that," he said.

"Thanks."

At home she wrote the paper in just under two hours. It was a record time for her, and she felt really pleased with the results. In addition to her interview with Kurt, she had consulted half a dozen books for her information. It was the last of her papers, and she was certain that it was the best.

When she was done, she called Tamara. "Want to go for some coffee or dessert?"

"I'd love to, but it's going to take me at least another five hours to write this paper," Tamara said with a sigh.

"That's okay. I have another question though."

"What?"

"I've been thinking about trying to switch a shift with someone so that I can attend one of the nights of Scare. I've heard you and my parents talk about how fun it was, and now I'm totally curious."

"You're not seriously going to ask me to put myself in a position to be frightened again, are you?"

"Actually, I am. I can't think of anyone else I'd rather scream like a little girl with."

Tamara laughed. "Well, when you put it that way, how can I refuse?"

"I was hoping you'd say that."

"Fine, I'll go. Just tell me when."

"Great. I'll see who I can bribe into switching with me."

Candace hung up and made her way back to the park, hoping to catch some of the regular cart vendors still on duty. She made a beeline for the cart storage area, hoping to run into someone. She found Martha and explained her mission.

"I'm sure Megan would love to switch," Martha said. "Her cart's currently in the Exploration Zone if you want to go ask her."

"Great, thanks!"

Candace had switched shifts with Megan before, over the summer. She hadn't realized the other girl was a regular referee instead of just seasonal.

The Exploration Zone was dominated by the Atomic Coaster, a roller coaster that looked like a giant atom. The zone was dedicated to science and exploration. Several buildings housed attractions and hands-on exhibits dedicated to astronomy, physics, geology, biology, archaeology, and chemistry. It was home to the Muffin Mansion kitchen, an experiment in chemistry if ever there was one. Candace found Megan in front of a huge building with a lifesize T-Rex apparently breaking out of it.

"Hey, what are you doing here?" Megan asked in surprise.

"Actually I was looking for you. I need to have one of the Scare nights off this weekend, and I wanted to know if you'd be willing to swap a Saturday or Sunday day shift."

"Would I ever! I work Saturday from nine to four. I'd love to switch it for the Saturday Scare shift."

"Awesome. Thank you."

"Not a problem. I should be thanking you. I'd love to be working Scare every night."

"Why aren't you?"

"They already had enough vendors signed up by the time I asked about it."

Candace felt bad for her. She wondered if they added an extra position for Candace when she was removed from the maze.

"That's too bad."

Megan shrugged. "If people keep quitting Scare, then I might get moved after all."

"People are quitting Scare?" Candace asked.

"Lots. They're scared of the ghost," Megan said.

Candace laughed. "That's silly. There's no such thing as ghosts."

"That's what I think. Lots of people are spooked though."

Since Candace didn't believe in ghosts, the real question seemed to be: Who was scaring the Scare referees?

"Thanks again. I'll put in the paperwork."

Megan nodded cheerfully, and Candace moved away. She was so deep in thought that she jumped, startled, when someone grabbed her shoulder.

"Hey, Candy."

It was Brandon.

"Where's your evil twin?" Candace snapped.

"Good one. Oh, Will is somewhere about."

"What do you want?" Candace asked.

"A date."

"No."

"Then a kiss," he leered.

"No! Get away from me. I have a boyfriend, and he'll take care of you."

"Ooh, I'm scared."

Candace saw a flash from the corner of her eye, and then a broom hit Brandon in the back of the head.

"Sorry," Sue said, smiling innocently. "I can be so clumsy sometimes."

Brandon muttered something under his breath before taking off.

"Thank you," Candace said.

"No problem."

"That's the third time someone has had to rescue me from that creep and his friend," Candace said.

"Next time you might want to try decking one of them," Sue suggested.

The idea had appeal, but Candace didn't know the first thing about fighting or punching. Plus what about turning the other cheek? She sighed. She was going to have to work it out, because she was pretty sure this wasn't the last she would see of Brandon and Will.

"Hey, I heard you're running Sugar Shock," Sue said, changing the subject.

"Helping to run it," Candace corrected. "Martha's the one in charge."

"Good luck with that. I think it's awesome, by the way, that you're helping out."

"Would you like to help out?" Candace asked. "We could use a few more refs working that day."

"Sorry. That is one day I'm definitely not working. I'm bringing my brother and sister to it."

"Cool! How old are they?"

"Gus is nine, and Mary is seven."

"Our target demographics," Candace said with a laugh.

"Tell me about it! Mom brought them last year, and they couldn't stop talking about it for weeks."

"Then I'll have to work doubly hard to make sure they're more impressed this year than last," Candace said.

"That would be great."

"Hey, I've got a question. Maybe you could answer it."

"What?"

"Why do they call it Sugar Shock?"

Sue smirked. "You ever seen several thousand kids jacked up on way too much sugar all at the same time all in the same place?"

"No," Candace admitted.

"Once you have, you'll understand."

Candace heard the train coming and out of reflex glanced toward the tracks to make sure she was well clear of them. What she did see turned her blood cold. A little boy was sitting on the tracks, licking an ice cream cone, oblivious to the oncoming train. The train blasted the horn several times in urgent succession.

Candace sprang forward into the path of the train and grabbed the boy. She saw Pete's face inside the engine, his eyes wide in terror, and she could tell that he was shouting something she couldn't hear.

She jumped off the tracks, falling as she did. She managed to twist so that the little boy landed on top of her. The ice cream cone went flying in the air and was obliterated by the train as it rushed by.

Candace scrambled to her feet, thrust the little boy at Sue, and took off after the train. Something was terribly wrong. When she caught up with the train, it was at rest fifty yards from the station. Security and at least two supervisors were on hand.

Pete was sitting on the ground beside his beloved train, his face ashen.

"I knew it! I told them to fire you, that one day you'd go too far and someone would really get hurt!" one of the supervisors was shouting.

"It wasn't his fault!" Candace interrupted.

All eyes turned on her. "I saw the whole thing. Pete wasn't trying to hurt the kid; he was just as frightened as the rest of us. I'd be willing to swear that this was no prank on his part," Candace said.

"What happened, Pete?" the other supervisor asked quietly.

Candace could see that Pete's hands were shaking. "The brakes failed," he said. "I don't know how, but they did. I couldn't stop. I just had to stay with her and let her run herself out," Pete said. "Is the boy all right?" he asked Candace.

"He is. I left him with Sue," Candace assured him.

"It's easy enough to check out," one of the security guards said, heading for the train.

Five minutes later he had confirmed that the brakes had malfunctioned. Satisfied, Candace turned to go, not wanting to stick around for the paperwork. Pete would be fine.

"Thank you," Pete called after her.

"Any time," she said. "Have them call me if they have any other questions."

As soon as she was out of earshot, she pulled out her cell. "Josh, it's Candace, can you meet me for coffee?"

Twenty minutes later she was in her favorite coffee shop with Josh. She was drinking her customary hot chocolate with a shot of raspberry. Josh was contenting himself with a hot cider with whipped cream. She finished telling him about the last hour.

"Wow," he said. "It's kind of weird how close you've been to so many accidents."

"I was thinking of something else," she said.

"I'm all ears."

"I don't believe that Scare is haunted."

"Neither do I. Unfortunately, fifteen people have quit in the last three days."

"I also think these accidents aren't accidents."

He leaned forward quickly, eyes narrowed. "I've been thinking the same thing myself."

Several things that had seemed like coincidences started falling together. What was it Tamara had said about there being no coincidences?

"In the Candy Craze maze right before that board came loose and hit me in the head, I thought I saw someone. It looked like a costumed character, but not one of the ones that belong in that maze. I had forgotten about it until now.

"Then I saw someone dressed like a fisherman with a hook on his hand go into the Haunted Village maze several minutes before the rest of the referees showed up. When security showed up after the girl was hurt, the fisherman was nowhere to be found."

"I heard something about that. It turned out the girl's ex had an alibi for that night. The police are still trying to figure out who did it."

She shuddered. "Thanks for warning me in a timely manner," she said sarcastically.

"Sorry," he said with a grimace. "Anyway, what about today before the train ran amok? Was there anyone out of place?"

"Actually, yes. Brandon. He only works Scare. There was no reason for him to be there, so close to the accident. Also, his friend Will wasn't there, and I've never seen one without the other."

"Suspicious, but not conclusive," Josh said.

"Who would benefit from convincing people that the park was haunted?" Candace asked.

"Competitors. There are three other theme parks within an hour's drive of here that put on Halloween events. The Zone's is the biggest, best, and by far the most popular. If it got out that The Zone was haunted, referees might quit."

"Just like they're quitting now," she pointed out. "And then?"

"If there weren't enough referees, some of the mazes would have to shut down."

"And suddenly word gets out that The Zone isn't the biggest and the best."

"And the players go elsewhere," Josh confirmed. "Worse, if the damage was extensive enough, the accidents numerous enough, it might extend beyond this Halloween. It might put The Zone out of the Halloween business all together."

"That sounds an awful lot like a motive to me," she said.

"The only question is, how do we prove it?"

"I have no idea. But I'd be willing to bet you a pizza that there are going to be more accidents this weekend."

"I'm betting you're right."

"I wonder if the targets are random, or if there is some kind of sense to it?"

"Well, going after you first makes perfect sense," Josh said.

"How?" she asked, startled.

"You were the star of the new maze, the flagship of this Scare. Better than that, you were the person the maze was designed around. Whoever loosened that board was probably hoping to either get the maze shut down or gain a great deal of publicity."

"They miscalculated," Candace said grimly.

"Which might explain why the attacks moved from the subtle to the more obvious. A maniac slashing a girl is a lot more news-worthy than a loose board causing a concussion."

"And the train today. Someone could have been seriously hurt or even killed." The thought sickened her. Would someone really go to such lengths to sabotage the Halloween events at The Zone?

"Candace, I've got a bad feeling about all this."

"So do I."

14

The next day at school, Candace thought she was having déjà vu. Everyone was staring and talking about her. She looked around suspiciously, but Tamara didn't seem to have hung any fresh banners.

She joined up with Tamara in homeroom where everyone continued to stare and whisper. "Do I have something on my face, or what?" Candace asked Tamara.

"I don't know what's going on," her best friend said, sounding just as puzzled as Candace. "But five people stopped me between my locker and here this morning to ask if my friend Candace worked at The Zone."

"What is this, delayed reaction? You hung that banner a couple of weeks ago."

"I know, it's kinda creepy. Either some people are just really slow, or something else is going on that we don't know about."

Candace was personally hoping people were slow. The other thought made her nervous.

Finally, a girl leaned forward and asked, "Candace, you worked at The Zone over the summer, right?"

"Yeah."

A dozen people started murmuring at that.

"What was your job?"

"I was a cotton candy vendor," Candace said.

This was followed by more murmuring.

"Were you locked in the theme park overnight?" the girl asked, eyes wide.

"Yes."

"I knew it!" The girl lurched to her feet and shouted, "Hey, everyone, it's true! Candace is Candy, the girl who got chased through the park by the psycho!"

The entire class erupted at that, and suddenly people were swarming around Candace's desk.

"What was it like?"

"Were you scared?"

"Do you have any scars?"

"How did you escape?"

"Is The Zone paying you like a billion dollars for your story?"

"None of that happened!" Candace tried to shout above the hubbub, but her voice was drowned out by the crowd.

She turned in desperation to Tamara. Her friend looked stunned but slowly began to laugh. "It's not funny!" Candace shouted.

"Are you sure?" Tamara shouted back.

Just great. The whole school had known she was *playing* Candy. Now apparently they realized she *was* Candy.

A group of guys started up a chorus of "I Want Candy," and she just groaned and put her head on the desk.

By the time drama class rolled around, the news was all over the school. Somehow, no matter what acting or improv task Mr. Bailey assigned to an individual or a group, cotton candy and psycho killers found their way into it. Fortunately they ran out of time, and she didn't have to get on stage to perform. She didn't think she could have handled it.

She'd been home only a few minutes when Pastor Bobby called. Candace was surprised. She had been called about retreats and things by some of the youth counselors before, but never by Pastor Bobby. Once the preliminaries were out of the way, he began.

"Candace, I just wanted to call because I have this concern."

And now everyone at church knows too. Just great.

"Let me just tell you right now that it never really happened. Yes, I was trapped in The Zone overnight. Yes, I was a cotton candy vendor all summer. No, there was no serial killer, no psycho, nothing like that."

"That was actually you?" he asked, sounding awed. "I knew you were playing the character in the maze, but I had no idea that story was based on you."

She groaned. Fabulous. Apparently it hadn't gotten around church quite yet, but it would now. "Why were you calling?" she asked.

"Oh, yes. I'm concerned that not enough juniors or seniors are going to volunteer to lead the small group Bible studies starting in November."

Thanks to Scare, she had missed the last couple youth group meetings, so she wasn't entirely sure what he was talking about. "Bible studies?"

"Yes, it's this new program we're trying out, and we need volunteers to lead and facilitate."

"And so you called me?"

"Yes."

"To volunteer?"

"Yes."

"Okay," she said, trying to gather her thoughts. It was probably going to be a big time commitment, and she wasn't sure she could handle it.

"Great, I knew I could count on you. See you Sunday!"

"Wait! I didn't mean 'okay, I'll do it—'"

It was too late, he had already hung up.

She thought about calling him right back, but she didn't. She had been learning firsthand how hard it was to get volunteers. Besides, it would look good on her college application. She sighed and hung up the phone. Hopefully Tamara could at least tell her something about what she had just volunteered for. In the meantime, she had some recruitment of her own to do.

"Come on, won't you volunteer … for me?" Candace asked, batting her eyelashes.

"No," Kurt said, smiling.

"No?"

"No."

She was surprised. She had figured the girlfriend card would trump the Halloween night card. Once the surprise faded, the disappointment set in.

"Seriously, you won't help me out?"

"Not with Sugar Shock," he said.

"Honestly, I don't get what the big deal is."

"That's because you've never worked Halloween night. It's long, it's exhausting, and people are lucky to survive—and that's if they managed to sleep all day in anticipation of it."

"Would it help if I begged?" she asked, thinking of Martha's advice.

"Not even a little bit. You'd just embarrass both of us."

She sighed in frustration before heading off to try and scare up some other volunteers. So far she had only four names on her list. Josh had agreed the night before to volunteer, and since then she had found only three other people willing to help. Of course, the truth was the overtime pay had enticed them and not the chance to entertain the kids.

She continued on through the History Zone, asking every referee she came across. Thirty minutes later she still didn't have a new name for her list. She headed for the Exploration Zone, hoping to find better luck there. No sooner had she stepped foot in the zone, than she saw Gib from the Muffin Mansion approaching her.

He looked grim, and she was reminded of when he had confronted her over the summer and told her about Becca's allergy to sugar and forbidden her to give Becca any more cotton candy.

He stopped in front of her, feet spread slightly apart, hands on his hips. He was already in costume. Everyone from the Muffin Mansion was a pirate. Candace had seen several of them walking around the park. They all looked good, but not like Gib. Gib, with his grim look and grizzled face, looked the part. He sounded a little like a pirate even when he wasn't in character, so it was easy to see him in the clothes and believe it.

"I've been looking for you, Candace," he grumbled.

"Sure, you've come to the proper place," Candace joked.

"I've been wanting to talk to you about your Sugar Shock."

It was hardly *her* Sugar Shock, but she figured it was best not to point that out. Clearly he had something to say, and she should let him say it.

"I hear you've been recruiting."

"You hear right," she said. What on earth could he want? Had he come to volunteer? Somehow she didn't think so.

"I'm here to give you a friendly warning. Don't recruit Becca."

She stared deep into his eyes and knew better than to ask if he was kidding. She knew about Becca's allergy to sugar and had seen firsthand how hyper it could make her. But surely Becca had to have some bit of self-control.

"She would only be passing out candy, not eating it."

"That's what you think."

"She must have a little self-control."

"None."

"But at the Muffin Mansion you put sugar in the muffins."

"And we keep that sugar locked up at all times. There's only one key," Gib said, hooking a finger under the chain around his neck and bringing into view the key in question. He lowered it back under his shirt, and Candace shivered.

"But the muffins have sugar in them. Surely she eats them."

"Only four types of muffins have real sugar in them. We also keep those locked up."

"That's insane! Why isn't she working at one of the rides instead?"

"She's Muffin Mansion crew, and we take care of our own. We don't need outside interference," Gib said, eyes blazing fiercely.

"Okay, fine, I won't ask her to work Sugar Shock."

"It's more than that. You have to swear to do everything in your power to keep her away from Sugar Shock."

"Okay, now that's just going too far," Candace protested. Muffin Mansion people might take care of their own, but she wasn't one of them, and she was not obligated to watch out for Becca.

Gib stepped closer, his manner subtly threatening. "You know how this event came to be named Sugar Shock?"

"No," Candace said. Could Gib actually have the answer to that?

"Twelve years ago, The Zone held its first Halloween event for children. They called it the Trick-or-Treat Zone."

That made a lot more sense to Candace than Sugar Shock.

"An unsuspecting relative brought a sweet, seven-year-old girl to that event, not knowing that the girl was allergic to sugar."

Gib had to be talking about Becca. The air seemed to grow suddenly colder, and Candace wrapped her arms around herself.

"The little girl trick-or-treated throughout the entire park, collecting an enormous bag of candy. And then she took the first bite," Gib said, his voice barely a whisper, his eyes fixed as though upon that moment so long ago.

"Three hours later they caught her," Gib said, his voice suddenly booming. "But by then she had cut a sugary swathe through seven zones, leaving carnage in her wake. She splattered the paints from the Painting Wall throughout the park and finally dumped the jars in the waters of the Splash Zone where they clogged up the machinery that kept the water and rides moving. Hundreds of players were stranded on rides throughout the park. The fire department was called. The police arrived. The park was evacuated. It took three of us from the Muffin Mansion to hold her when we finally caught her. I still bear the scars," Gib said, rolling up the sleeve of his left arm.

"Are those bite marks?" Candace asked in horror.

"Aye. She left her mark on each of us. And we vowed on that day to never let her step foot inside this park if she could reach sugar again. Little Becca spent two days in the hospital recovering from the shock of the sugar. The park spent two weeks recovering from the shock of the events and repairing the damage. And that's why we call it Sugar Shock."

Candace just stared at him in horror. So many questions were racing through her mind. All she knew for certain was that The Zone had to be a magical place for that little girl to ever want to come back and for those brave, tormented referees to welcome her with open arms. If that wasn't love, she didn't know what was.

"The Muffin Mansion takes care of its own," she whispered.

"Aye."

Candace was starting to get desperate when she headed for the Game Zone. She had managed to get only a couple more volunteers, and she was running out of options.

She walked into the Dug Out and found Roger there.

"What are you doing here? I thought you were just working Scare," she said, confused.

He indicated to her that he was not wearing a uniform. "I'm here as a player. I'm buying my cousin a birthday present."

"Oh, cool. Can I talk to you for a second?"

"Sure, what's up?"

"I don't know if you've heard, but I'm helping to run Sugar Shock this year."

"I did hear. That's totally cool."

"You know what would be even cooler?"

"What?"

"If you volunteered to work it."

"Okay."

"Really?" she asked, surprised.

"Yes."

"Thank you! That would be awesome!"

"Having a hard time getting people to say yes?"

"How'd you guess?"

"Word gets around."

"Has word gotten around about anybody who might be willing to volunteer?" she asked hopefully.

"No. I'll make you a deal, though," he said.

"What?"

Suddenly he started blushing fiercely. "I'll get you nine other guys if you find out for me if Becca has a boyfriend."

"Seriously?" Candace asked.

"Yeah."

"Deal," she said, shaking his hand.

She didn't know which amazed her more, that he would ask her to find out if Becca had a boyfriend, which felt like a very third-grade request to her, or that he would volunteer nine of his friends for the information.

She went immediately to the Muffin Mansion to track down Becca. She found her and the other pirates in high spirits as they were getting ready for the evening to start.

"Hey, Candace!" Becca said, waving furiously.

"Hey, Becca. Can I see you a sec?"

Becca came over. "What's up?"

"I'm not going to beat around the bush. Someone asked me to find out if you have a boyfriend."

Becca smiled. "That's valuable information. What are they offering in exchange for it?"

"Nine of their friends as volunteers for Sugar Shock."

Becca's eyes went wide. "Nine?"

"Nine," Candace confirmed.

"You can tell this person that I don't have a boyfriend."

"Do you want to know who's asking?" Candace said.

"No," Becca said with an impish smile. "It's more fun this way."

"If you say so," Candace said, shaking her head. "Thanks for the information."

"You're welcome," Becca said before disappearing back into the pirate horde.

Eager to seal the deal, Candace hurried back to the Game Zone where she found Roger right before he entered the maze. "Roger!"

"Yes?" he asked, looking nervous.

"No boyfriend."

He broke out into a huge grin. "You're sure?"

"I'm sure. You owe me nine other volunteers."

"You'll have them," he assured her.

Candace headed for the castle. Now, if only she could find a few other people willing to volunteer their friends, she'd be doing well.

Once inside the Comfort Zone, she taped her list of names to one of the walls.

"It's a start," Martha said when she perused the list a few minutes later.

"So, what's supposed to happen at Sugar Shock?" Candace asked.

"Generally only a few rides are open. Referees are stationed throughout the park at tables with big bowls of candy they pass out to the trick-or-treaters."

"That's it?"

"Isn't that enough?" Martha asked. "We have a hard enough time pulling just that off every year."

"Doesn't Freddie McFly make an appearance?"

"Yeah, he and Mr. Nine Lives do a walk around, signing autographs. Plus they do a little improv show."

"Not a big show?"

Martha shook her head. "They do the big show on Scare nights, so they have to save their energy for that."

"Well, that's sad."

Martha shrugged. "Sugar Shock is more of the afterthought of the holiday. Most of the time, money, and personnel gets funneled into Scare."

"Speaking of money, do we have any so that we could buy props or stuff besides candy?"

"A little. Why? What are you thinking?"

"I know we don't have a lot of time, but I think this year Sugar Shock needs to be more of an event than an afterthought."

"Just tell me what you want to do," Martha said.

15

Candace was waiting when the train rolled into the station. Pete opened the door of the engine and looked down at her first in surprise and then in resignation. She knew he was taking the train on a test run to check the repaired brakes, and she had waited for just this moment.

"You know why I'm here," Candace said, locking eyes with him.

"Yeah, I reckon I do," he said with a heavy sigh.

"You had to know this day was coming," she continued.

"I'd have been a fool not to," he said.

"And nobody takes you for a fool, Pete."

"What do I have to do?"

"Run the train. Pass out candy."

"Is that it?"

"That's enough," she said.

"All right then."

"All right." He climbed back aboard the train and pulled slowly out of the station.

"That's one more happy volunteer," Candace said to herself. She had already secured quite a few.

She moved on, heading for her next scheduled stop. Dealing with Roger had taught her something. People would volunteer for a price. Know their price and you had them. It was pretty mercenary, but she had the Halloween dreams of little kids to fulfill and very little time to do it.

She checked the schedule printout in her hand and made her way to the Thrill Zone. Once there, it was easy to find the cart she was looking for.

"Megan," Candace said, as she approached the candy corn vendor.

"Yes?" Megan asked.

"How would you like to work the rest of Scare as a vendor?" Candace asked.

"Do you mean it?" Megan asked excitedly.

"Yes. You can work the remaining nights of Scare."

"That would be awesome! What's the catch?"

Candace smiled. "You have to volunteer to work Sugar Shock."

Megan's smile faltered for a moment, but was soon back in place. "You have yourself a deal."

"Great, finish your shift today, then report to cart storage tomorrow night at six thirty."

Megan gave her a brief salute, and Candace turned away to hide her smile. Martha and Candace had worked it out that Megan could take Candace's hours since Candace was going to have to put in so much time to finish organizing Sugar Shock. This way, everyone won.

She checked her list and headed for the Exploration Zone.

Gib was locking the door of the Muffin Mansion when Candace made her presence known. She cleared her throat loudly, and he turned to look at her in surprise.

"Candace?"

"Gib, I'm going to be straight with you, because you've always been straight with me."

He paled as though he sensed what was coming.

"I need five more volunteers."

"That does sound like a problem," he said, fidgeting.

"It is. A big problem. I need to find five volunteers some-place. Either that or I need one volunteer with the strength of five," she said meaningfully.

He turned even paler and lowered his gaze. "I'll get you five," he said, in a whisper.

"I appreciate that, Gib. And I'm sure I speak on behalf of the entire park when I say thank you."

He nodded and she went on her way.

Now that she had all her volunteers, there was only one nag-ging thought left. Would any of them actually show?

🍁

Candace awoke with a start. It was Friday morning, and she had just fallen asleep for the third time while taking her history test. She yawned and picked up her pencil off the ground yet again. She glanced up to see her teacher scowling at her. She ducked her head and continued on with her test.

She finished just before the bell rang. After she turned it in, she brought her permission slip to the front of the class. His was the only signature she had left to get. Sugar Shock was a day event, and in order to be there she would have to miss school. So far only one of her teachers had even bothered to look at the paper before signing it.

He took the paper and read it over. His perpetual scowl deepened, and he looked at her over the rims of his glasses.

"School is more important than Halloween," he lectured her.

"But, it's for my job. I'm in charge of one of the Halloween events at The Zone," she explained.

"A theme park. Such foolishness. It would be better if you got a job as a secretary, somewhere where you could learn real skills that mean something."

She folded her arms across her chest. His was the last signa-ture she needed, and she wasn't about to let a cranky, creaky history teacher get in her way.

"You know that Colonial America paper of mine that you liked so well?"

"Yes! Fine piece of work, good research. That's the kind of thing you should be focusing on."

"You know where I got all my information?"

He shook his head.

"The History Zone."

She stared into his eyes. He looked away first. He cleared his throat awkwardly. "You know, I haven't been to a theme park since I was a boy. Maybe it's time to go again."

"I would be happy to give you a tour of the entire History Zone," she said.

He signed her paper and handed it to her. "Good luck running your event. I just might take you up on that offer one of these days."

"That would be fine," she said. "Have a good evening."

"You too," he said, still not looking her in the eyes.

"Thank you," she said. She turned and left the classroom. Once outside she realized that her heart was pounding and her hands were shaking. She had done it though. She had all the signatures she needed.

"Sugar Shock, here I come."

🍁

On Saturday night it felt weird to show up at the park as a player instead of a referee. Candace's excitement was tempered by the realization that there was likely going to be another accident soon. She hadn't heard of anything happening the previous two nights, which only made her worry more.

Still, her fears slipped into the background as she and Tamara stepped into the fog-shrouded world of Scare. Candace realized that she must have finally become acclimated to the fog, because it no longer made her cough.

As they walked through the park, monsters charged them from out of the dark, seeing how close they could get without actually touching. Tamara jumped every time, but Candace found herself too busy with trying to figure out who was who under the masks to let herself get really scared.

"Which maze should we start with?" Candace asked Tamara.

"Screen Screams was really good," Tamara said reluctantly.

Candace appreciated the fact that Tam was putting herself through this to keep her company. Apparently her first Scare hadn't anesthetized her at all; she still jumped at every sound or flicker of movement. Fortunately there was only a five-minute line for Screen Screams.

While they waited, they talked.

"You're asking Kurt to the Winter Formal, right?" Tamara asked.

"That's the plan," Candace said. "How about you?"

"I don't know who I'm going to go with. I might wait for someone to ask me."

"Or you could ask someone that doesn't go to our school, like Josh maybe."

Tamara rolled her eyes. "Lay off already. I've told you, I like Josh. It's just not right though. We're not going to get together no matter how much you like the idea of setting us up."

"Can't blame a girl for trying," Candace said with a sigh.

"I guess not."

"Okay, no more trying to set up you and Josh."

"Thank you."

"How about Roger?"

Tamara hit her playfully in the arm.

Candace grinned. "Okay, no setting you up with anyone. I get it."

"Good."

"The pirates are loose!" a referee ran by yelling.

"What on earth?" Candace wondered.

A second referee was on his heels. "What's happening?" Candace called.

The man slowed up for a moment. "The pirates have taken over the Haunted Village."

"Are you kidding me?" Candace asked.

"No. They descended like a horde and overran the maze. They raised their flag, and they have a ship in the lighthouse lagoon."

The man looked genuinely freaked out. She recognized him as one of the characters from the Haunted Village maze. "Why would they do that?" she asked.

"Because they're pirates!" he said, as though it was the dumbest question he had ever heard. He continued running.

"Okay, I think we have to go see that next," Tamara said. "That just sounds cool."

"It sounds bizarre," Candace said.

They reached the front of the Screen Screams line and were soon let inside. The entire maze was themed after horror movies, both classic and modern. Everything from Hitchcock to Michael Myers was represented. Candace hadn't seen a lot of horror films but was still able to recognize what most of them were.

Tamara kept screaming and digging her fingernails into Candace's arm and shoulder. She was certain her friend had drawn blood. Candace yelped as a guy in a Scream mask jumped out at them. Some high-tech optical illusions and rubber props made it look like the next room was crawling with rats.

Tamara came to an abrupt stop, practically pulling Candace's arm from its socket.

"You've already been through here. They're fake!" Candace said.

Tamara whimpered and shook her head.

Candace saw something move out of the corner of her eye. It looked like one of the mummies, but she couldn't be sure. A chill slid up her spine, and she turned back to look at the room in front of them. It was then that she realized that some of the rats were real.

Candace screamed and backed up, pushing Tamara behind her. The guy in the Scream mask hesitated, unsure what was happening. Candace seized him. "Get an umpire now! There are real rats in the next room."

The guy took off, and a minute later umpires were clearing the maze. Security guards showed up, and once again Candace found herself explaining what had happened. As soon as they were finished, Candace put her arm around Tamara, who was still shaking, and dragged her over to the castle.

She sent a message into the Dracula maze, and a minute later Josh appeared. He and Tamara followed her down the side of the castle, and she let them all in through the secret door and upstairs to the Comfort Zone. If anyone needed comforting, it was her and Tamara. Besides, she couldn't think of a better place for a private conversation.

She got them sodas from the vending machine, and they sat on the couches. Candace quickly filled Josh in on what had just happened.

"You're right," he said grimly when she had finished her story. "There's no way something like that is an accident."

"And I'm just betting Will and Brandon are behind this. They put a live mouse on me in the costume area a couple of weeks ago."

"I think they're after you," Tamara said quietly.

"What?"

"I think they've been spying on you."

"It does make sense. These things seem to happen when you're around," Josh said.

"But, how did they know I would go into that maze tonight?"

"They probably knew you were going to be here as a player and were hoping you would. They watched, and when you did—instant rat attack."

Candace shivered. "But I haven't been present for all the attacks, and they haven't all been directed toward me."

"The only one you weren't present for was in Kurt's maze. That wall could have seriously hurt him when it fell," Josh said. "I'd say someone wanted to send a warning to your boyfriend."

"I don't believe this."

"Why?" Tamara asked. "You are the ultimate symbol of this year's Scare."

"But I haven't even been in that maze since the first weekend!"

"No, but the urban legend started with you," Josh said.

"If this is true, how can we stop it?" she asked.

"They're going to want to strike again soon. They need something big to make sure Scare closes before next weekend."

"Great, so how do we know what they're going to do?" Candace asked. "I mean, the thing with the hook was pretty major, and it didn't do the trick. What more could they have in mind that would be bigger?"

"Until now no one's really gotten hurt. At least, not badly," Tamara said.

"I don't think we can count on it to stay that way," Josh said grimly.

Candace's head was spinning. What they were talking about was insane, but deep down she knew it was true. She had never bought the whole "ghost" thing, and too many of the incidents seemed to have happened when she was around. She was just grateful that people weren't pointing a finger in her direction.

"So, what do we do?" Candace asked.

"I think it's time to call in a supervisor," Josh said.

"Then it looks like I'm right on time," Martha said from the doorway.

All three of them jumped. They had been so intent on their conversation they hadn't heard her come in.

"How long have you been there?" Candace asked.

"Long enough," Martha said grimly. "I think all of you are right, but we're going to have to catch them in the act."

"How?" Josh queried.

"We set our own trap. I'll spread the word that Lisa sprained her ankle tonight, and tomorrow night our famed Candy reprises her role."

"You'd use Candace as bait?" Tamara asked.

Martha nodded. "I'll have security standing by. When they try to sabotage the maze, we'll catch them."

"No way!" Josh said, jumping up. "We can't risk Candace like that."

"Martha's right," Candace said. A frightened, miserable feeling settled in the pit of her stomach. "If they have this weird obsession with doing things while I'm around, the best way to catch them is to make sure that I'm right back where I started when things first went wrong."

"It makes a lot of sense," Tamara admitted.

"The fewer people who know about this the better. Candace, come tomorrow night prepared to get back in the role," Martha said.

Josh looked frustrated, but Candace could tell that he didn't have a better solution.

"Okay," Candace said. "Let's catch some bad guys."

16

"Let's catch some bad guys" has to be the worst final words ever, Candace thought. As she once again donned the Candy costume, she wasn't just nervous, she was terrified. God, please protect me and all of us. Please help us to catch the people responsible for this and help no one get hurt, she prayed. There was so much else that she wanted to say, but she just didn't have the words.

They needed to catch the saboteurs, but she wished they could have found some other way. Tamara was right, though, they did seem to have a particular interest in performing for Candace.

Tamara had tried to insist on being there, but Candace had convinced her to stay home, because the saboteurs would probably recognize her from the other night. Since she didn't work for The Zone, there was no way for her to blend into the background.

As Candace walked to the maze, she tried hard to calm herself down. It wasn't easy. All around her other referees waved and congratulated her on her return to the mazes. When she reached Candy Craze, both Ray and Reggie welcomed her back and assured her that no matter what anybody said, there was only one Candy, and she was it.

She appreciated their support and words of encouragement. She wished she could tell them what was happening, but the fewer people who knew what was going on the better.

The music and fog started up. She and Reggie took their starting positions. When the first players came through, Candace jumped in front of them and then ran. She made it all the way through the different parts of the maze and returned to the beginning, marveling at how it felt like she had never left.

On her second run through she had the satisfaction of seeing a couple of grown men screaming like five-year-olds. She began to loosen up. Reggie and Ray were both in fine form too, really giving a hundred percent each time.

"Did you hear about the pirates marauding last night?" Reggie asked at one point.

"Only a little. Tell me about it," Candace said before jumping out and running.

When she returned to the starting place, Reggie continued. "They kicked all the maze characters out of the Haunted Village and claimed it as their own."

"You're kidding," Candace said on her return. It was a strange way to hold a conversation, but it was kind of fun.

"Nope. They've taken over the entire Splash Zone, and word is that's just the beginning of their plans."

"That I've gotta see," Candace said before starting to run again.

"How do they get away with that?" she asked when she returned.

"It's a special thing. Each year a different group is selected to do special things. They get a lot more freedom than the rest of us."

"Cool! How do they pick the team?" Candace just had time to ask.

"It's based on performance throughout the year," Reggie explained a couple minutes later. "The winning team sits down with the owner of the park and picks their theme."

Candace jumped out and had to start running again before she had a chance to ask anything else. As she ran through the maze, she imagined how cool that would be. She also wondered just what the pirates' limits were. It seemed strange, but it fit in with everything else she knew about The Zone.

The group that was following on her heels was a particularly noisy one made up of all different ages. She swore she recognized some of them from earlier performances. She had heard that some players came to every single night of Scare. She was starting to believe it.

She made it to the finale, and Ray caught her. She struggled hard, trying to give the group a good show. Ray's arm tightened painfully across her chest, though, and his fingers were digging into her arm. She winced in pain.

"Ray, you're hurting me," she said, just loud enough for him to hear.

"Not Ray," a male voice hissed back.

Fear shot through her. It had happened. She had dropped her guard just enough. The saboteurs had come for her, and everyone would think it was just part of the show. "Help me!" she screamed.

He chuckled in her ear. "Nobody's coming to help you. In fact, they're going to be too busy trying to sort out the mummy mess to think about you for quite a while."

It was Brandon's voice. She was sure of it. Through her mind flashed every time he and his friend had tormented her in the past few weeks. The first meeting, the mouse, by the train tracks. Each time someone had shown up to save her. This time, though, nobody was coming. Josh was in his maze across the park, and Kurt and Sue didn't even know that Candace was being used as bait.

What would Dad do? she asked herself. When she was a little girl, he had told her how to protect herself. What would he do now?

Candace jammed her heel down on his instep. He groaned and loosened his grip ever so slightly. She spun around and jabbed her fingers toward his eyes. Backing away, he tripped. An umpire appeared suddenly with another psycho, and together they tackled the fallen man.

"Got you!" she heard the second psycho yell. He sounded like the real Ray.

Ray and the umpire struggled against Brandon, but she didn't have time to help. What was it Brandon had said about the mummy mess?

Candace turned and ran outside, leading the cheering players out and to safety. She stopped the security guard just outside. "Radio Martha and tell her that one of the bad guys is in the Mummy's Curse maze! Then get inside and help subdue the other guy!"

He grabbed the radio, and she could hear him relaying her message even as she began to run. She had no idea what she was doing. From what Brandon had said, it might already be too late. Even if she did get there in time, how would she find Will?

A golf cart suddenly roared up beside her, its honk sounding like the whistle of a train. Pete was driving. "Jump on! I can get you there faster!"

She jumped. One foot anchored safely on the cart, and she swung the rest of herself in as Pete hit the gas. She was flung back in her seat as they went flying forward. The whistlelike horn blew continuously, and players and referees scattered before them.

"I need to get to the Mummy's Curse!" she shouted.

"I know!" he said.

The golf cart was moving at impossibly high speeds. Suddenly it rocketed ahead, and the wind whipping by brought tears to her eyes.

"I made a lot of special modifications myself!" Pete shouted.

Of course he did. She wondered briefly why he wasn't one of the pirate crew.

The pyramids of Egypt loomed in front of them, and Pete drove right up to the exit of the one holding the maze. A man in a vampire costume was just coming out. For a brief moment she thought it was Josh, but when the guy saw her he started to run. Candace leaped off the cart and tried to grab him. He twisted out of her reach, and disappeared back inside the maze.

Without thinking, Candace charged in after him. She saw the edge of his cloak disappear down a right-hand turn.

A maze, why did it have to be a maze? And worst of all, it was the only maze in the park that was an actual maze. She skidded to a stop when the hallway divided itself again. After a moment's hesitation, she turned left, guessing that he would have chosen that rather than risk running straight a little bit farther.

The maze was lit by flickering torches, which had the effect of making the painted hieroglyphics on the wall seem to move. Soon she was lost deep inside the maze. She ran into several groups of people just as lost as she was. To each of them she shouted, "Have you seen a vampire in here?"

All but one man looked at her like she was crazy. That man pointed down a dark tunnel.

Candace plunged into the tunnel and instantly realized she had made a mistake. The torchlight in this section was almost nonexistent. The sounds of players faded into the distance. Reason told her that she was never going to find Will in the endless web of tunnels and passageways. She should get herself out before whatever booby trap he had rigged went off.

She remembered what Josh had said about Will and Brandon upping the stakes. Whatever they had planned was probably going to be a lot more dangerous.

She turned back, but it was dark behind her and she knew she wouldn't recognize the path she had taken. Fear gripped her. She was lost with no way out. In the distance she heard shouts. She only hoped it was security clearing the maze and that they would find her soon. She thought about shouting for someone to find her.

Before she could decide what to do, she heard another sound coming from a few feet ahead. It was just a whisper, like a cape rustling against the floor. She held her breath and inched her way forward, praying that her eyes would adjust to the low lighting. Then she heard him breathing, hard. Whoever it was had been running.

She stayed absolutely still, trying not to make a sound that would give her away. The shouts were getting louder. She wondered how long before they found her. The more she thought about it, she realized she had been crazy to chase him in here. She hadn't thought, just acted. What was she going to do if she caught him?

Suddenly she thought of a much more grisly possibility. What would happen if he caught her?

"I see you," Will said suddenly.

Candace jerked but didn't make a sound. Maybe it was a bluff to try to get her to expose herself. With any luck Will couldn't see any better in the dark than she could. Her heart was pounding even faster now than it had been before. She could feel the bruises that Brandon had left in their struggle.

She heard Will start to walk slowly toward her. She retreated, putting one foot silently behind the other without turning her back to him. Her hand ran lightly along the wall, guiding her.

"They paid us a lot of money to sabotage Scare. Told us they didn't care how, just to get it done. We figured the best way to crush morale was to hurt the darling of the park."

Candace would hardly have called herself that. Still, in their twisted minds they probably believed the urban legend as much as the crazy Game Master Tish did.

The wall disappeared beneath her fingers, indicating a side passageway. She took it, still trying to move without making a sound. She could hear people coming closer. She just hoped Will wasn't paying attention. Maybe if she could keep just out of reach long enough, help would arrive.

Suddenly there was a rush of movement as he swung his arm toward her. She didn't let herself make a sound but continued to back up steadily. It had been a wild swing. He couldn't see anymore than she could.

She took another step back, and suddenly lights blazed on all around them. She froze for a moment, half-blinded, and stared in horror at Will who was also staring at her. The moment passed and Candace turned, fleeing up the narrow passageway.

She could hear his feet pounding on the ground behind her, and it spurred her on faster and faster. She plunged down one corridor and then crossed to another, hoping beyond hope that she was making her way toward either the exit or the entrance.

As fast as she ran, he was still gaining on her. She could hear him panting and feel the wind from his fingers as they passed by her time and again. She started to turn a corner only to realize it was a dead end. She lurched back into the main passageway, and she felt Will's hand come down on her shoulder. She twisted and plunged forward. There was a ripping sound as he tore her sleeve. She rounded another corner and ran headlong into a security guard.

He caught her with a grunt, and the two half fell against a wall. When Candace staggered back to her feet, she saw two other guards wrestling Will to the ground.

"We would have gotten away with it too, if it hadn't been for you and your stupid friends," he said.

"He did something to the maze!" she said.

"We already cleared out all the players," the first guard said. "His pal told us what to look for. Everything's going to be okay." He placed a hand on her shoulder, and she shied away from it. He backed up a step, holding both hands chest high.

"Are you okay?" he asked.

"No," Candace said. Her head was spinning, and sweat was pouring off her. In the bright light that now flooded the maze, she could see the bruises on her arms. And long scratch marks on her shoulder were bleeding. The Candy costume had lost its sleeve, making it even more grotesque looking.

The two other guards had subdued Will. The first guard called in on the radio. "We found them. We're in the main corridor."

"How far are we from an exit?" Candace asked.

"You're in the dead center of the maze," the guard said, then grimaced at his own choice of words.

"I'd like to leave now," she said.

She heard voices and more pounding feet. Then Pete, Martha, and Josh appeared. Pete was the first to reach her, and he hugged her hard.

"I followed you in, but I couldn't find you," he said.

"Thanks for trying," she said.

Josh shrugged out of his own cape and draped it around her shoulders.

An hour later the police took away Will and Brandon. They had confessed everything and had fingered the executive of the rival theme park who had hired them.

Josh finally came to sit beside Candace outside the maze.

"You okay?" he asked.

She nodded slowly.

It was strange to think that through the rest of the park players and referees alike continued about their revelries, unaware of the drama that had unfolded such a short distance away.

"A lot of excitement around here tonight," Josh joked. "I wonder if you heard about it?"

She smiled at his attempt at humor.

"You know what the funniest part is?"

"What?"

"This isn't even the end of Scare. I mean, next weekend is the big weekend."

"That is weird. We caught the bad guys. If this were a movie this would be Halloween."

"But it's not, and you know why that's great?" Josh asked.

"Because the bad guys didn't ruin everyone's Halloween?"

"Exactly. And who knows, once word gets out, you might have a lot more people volunteering to help you with Sugar Shock."

"That would be great," she said. "We're always looking for fresh victim—er, volunteers."

"At least you haven't lost your sense of humor."

"Yeah."

"I'm really proud of you. I know how much you hate mazes."

"I don't know what I was thinking," she admitted.

Another thought occurred to her. "How did Pete just happen to be there with a golf cart when I needed him?"

"Turns out he's been monitoring the security channel ever since the incident with his train. He was privy to our plan all night and was close by your maze in case there was trouble. When he heard the guard radio in about the Mummy Craze, he figured you could use help getting across the park fast."

"He was right."

"Hey, I know something that will lift your spirits."

"What's that?"

"Let's go watch the pirates in action."

Candace followed him toward the Splash Zone.

Before they got there, they saw the pirates in a group. Between them and the pirates was a figure in a gray suit that Candace recognized as Tish. Just then, Tish looked up from a clipboard and saw the pirates.

The pirates saw Tish. A great roar went up from their midst, and suddenly they descended on her. She screamed and turned to run, but was caught, as if in a tide, and tossed up into the air. Candace watched amazed as she was tossed back and forth, screaming the whole while. When she finally came back to earth, she was completely disheveled and someone had sprayed her hair green.

"Enough!" she screamed, turning to face the pirate horde.

Candace watched with bated breath as Tish tried to stare down the pirates.

"What say ye?" Gib shouted suddenly.

Becca surged to the front of the group. "Make her walk the plank!"

The pirates surged forward and seized Tish. Then they took off at a run toward the Splash Zone.

Candace followed at a distance, curiosity burning within her. When they reached the Splash Zone, Candace saw with amazement that there was a miniature pirate ship moored in the lake with the lighthouse. The pirates surged on board with their prize. They set Tish down at the edge of an actual plank that jutted off the side of the ship over the lake and then retreated a couple of steps, leaving her and Gib alone at the edge.

"I won't walk the plank!" the woman said, crossing her arms across her chest.

"Argh. That's okay, you don't have to if you don't want," Gib said and promptly pushed her.

Tish fell, screaming, and landed with a loud splash. The pirates gave a lusty cheer, and Candace joined them. Tish swam to the lighthouse and pulled herself up out of the water. She shook her fist at the pirates, which just made them cheer the louder.

Candace threw back her head and laughed. The pirates suddenly came swarming back off the boat, and Candace realized it was time to disappear before they made her walk the plank.

She wasn't sure if she could run anymore that night, but Josh pulled her into the shadow of a building and the pirates ran past.

"Wow, they really are marauding," she said in admiration. "And it's permissible?"

Josh nodded. "John Hanson believes that the closer it gets to Halloween, the more unexpected things should be for the referees. He's always figured that a little fear goes a long way toward enhancing performance and providing fun. Of course, I don't think he ever envisioned what happened to you tonight."

Candace shook her head. "Who could have? Honestly, I think it's cool that they get carte blanche to roam the park and cause mayhem. It makes me wish I was one of them."

"And give up being Candy?" he asked.

"Yes! Lisa can have it back next weekend. I'll be happy to go back to cart five. I've had my share of being chased for the time being."

"Just think, next time someone asks you if you've been chased through the park by a psycho, you can say yes," Josh said.

"Yeah, I guess I can," Candace said. "What do you know, something good came out of this after all."

"It usually does. You just have to look hard enough."

It was just absurd enough that she had to laugh.

17

Tamara and Candace had gotten in some much-needed rest and relaxation in the form of shopping after school on Monday. They made it back to Tamara's house with their packages and had strewn them all over the living room to inspect the damage.

"So are you sure you didn't have nightmares all night?" Tamara asked again.

"No, I guess I was so tired I just crashed."

"I still can't believe you did all that. You're a hero."

Candace grimaced. "That's not the word I would use."

"That's because you're still in denial over that whole spotlight thing."

"You're never going to give that a rest, are you?"

"Not until you admit that the spotlight is your friend."

It was good to be hanging with Tamara and teasing each other. It had been a great afternoon, but Candace found herself unable to stop thinking about the night before. And for some reason, thoughts of that seeemed to trigger questions about what she wanted to do with her life. Chief among her concerns at the moment was what she was going to do about college and a career choice.

"Tam, what do you want to do with your life?" Candace asked.

"Have fun," Tam said, smiling.

Candace rolled her eyes. "That much is obvious. I mean, what do you want to be?"

"The light operator shining that big old spotlight on you?"

"Seriously."

"Okay fine." Tamara looked thoughtful. "That's a hard question. When I was little I thought I wanted to be a doctor, but then I realized I'd have to deal with blood." She shuddered. "In middle school I thought about being a poet, until I realized I really didn't have anything to say. The more I watch my mom, the more I think I want to be like her. She doesn't have a job. She runs the family, does the entertaining, and takes care of all the social stuff so that my father doesn't have to deal with it. She also helps him with his business and does a lot of charity work. I have to say, that appeals to me."

"Really?" Candace asked, somewhat surprised.

"Yeah. I mean, I have plenty of time to change my mind, but right now I'm thinking that I want to be a society wife."

"How very Jackie Collins," Candace quipped.

"Please, nothing so torrid," Tamara said, rolling her eyes. "I think I would do well as the wife of an executive or a politician."

"So, instead of focusing on getting a BA, you're more interested in getting a MRS."

"That's funny," Tamara said, laughing. "I like that a lot. My MRS."

"I have a hard time seeing you married."

"Why? I'd be totally good at it."

"Probably because we're not even eighteen yet."

"Oh, like you don't think about marriage," Tamara retorted.

"Not very often."

"You don't think about marrying Kurt?"

"I think about not marrying Kurt," Candace said.

"Trouble in paradise?"

"No. It just feels awkward sometimes."

"Hello? What relationship doesn't?" Tamara asked.

"How would I know? This is my first boyfriend, remember? You've had, what, eight?"

"Please."

"Okay, how many?"

"Nine."

Candace snorted.

"Listen, Cand. If you want to break up with him, do it before one of you gets really hurt."

"But I don't want to break up with him," Candace protested.

"Then don't."

"I won't."

"Good. Glad we got that cleared up. Now we can talk about something really important."

"Like what?" Candace asked.

"Like what you're wearing to his Halloween party Wednesday night."

Candace smiled. "That is important. I could definitely use some help deciding on that."

"So, what are your thoughts?"

"It should be someone historical. He loves history."

"Any particular area?"

"No, pretty much all of it from what I can tell."

"I've got it!" Tamara exclaimed.

"What?"

"Where did you have your first romantic dinner?"

"Aphrodite's," Candace said, smiling at the memory. "Tam, you're a genius!"

"I know. Who do you love?"

"You."

"Not as much as you will in a minute."

"And why's that?"

"I've got the perfect Aphrodite costume for you."

Candace squealed and hugged Tamara. "You're right, I love you even more than a minute ago."

"Told you."

The events of Sunday night were already legend by Tuesday. Candace fielded a dozen phone calls from referees, and for once she was able to confirm the rumors instead of deny them.

Josh had also been right. Dozens of people were volunteering to work Sugar Shock. "One hundred and fifty volunteers," Martha said when she finished tallying them all on Tuesday afternoon.

"Wow! That many?" Candace asked, craning her neck to get a better look at the list.

"Yes. I have no idea what we're going to do with them all," Martha admitted.

"I do," Candace said. "I think we need to buy more candy."

"Check."

"And while we're at it, I think we need to organize a costume contest with prizes. We should also have Freddie McFly and Mr. Nine Lives lead a parade through the park."

"At this point I pretty much think whatever you want you're going to get," Martha said. "You're the girl who saved Scare. No one's going to deny you anything."

"Ah, the power! Must use it wisely." Candace pantomimed struggling to hold herself back.

Martha laughed. "Enjoy it while it lasts."

Candace heard the secret door downstairs open and waited curiously to see who was coming to the Comfort Zone. When the door at the top of the stairs opened, she was shocked to see the Zone's owner, John Hanson.

Martha stood up. "This is my cue to go buy that extra candy. I'm sure the two of you have a lot to talk about."

"Thanks, Martha," John said as she left.

The former quarterback settled down into the chair opposite Candace. "It seems that, once again, I am in your debt," he said by way of greeting.

Candace blushed. "Just doing my job," she mumbled.

"Volunteering to help run Sugar Shock. Exposing and capturing saboteurs intent on ruining this park's reputation. Risking yourself in that endeavor. None of those are in your job description. I know, I checked," he said with a smile.

Candace shrugged, at a loss for words.

"So, the question before me is what to do with you, Candace."

"What do you mean?"

"Very few people have had the impact on this park that you've had. You've worked for two seasons as a temporary employee. And both seasons have seen profound benefits to this park through your efforts."

"The Zone has given me a lot as well," she said. "Great friends and growth experiences."

"Indeed," he said with a smile. "Candace, I don't believe in coincidences."

She couldn't help but smile at that.

"I believe that God has brought you here for a reason. Therefore, it is my duty to discover how I may be of service in whatever plan it is that He has."

"I didn't know you were a Christian," she said.

He shrugged. "I make no secret of it. I wrote about my faith extensively in my autobiography. I guess I'm surprised when people are surprised."

"Sorry," she said.

"Not your fault. I must ask, though, do you know why God has brought you to us?"

She shook her head. "I'm not sure. I know that I've grown a lot through my experiences here. Maybe that's why."

"It's possible, but there are dozens of places where you could have grown and received life experience. I think there may be something more specific."

She was at a complete loss as to what to say. Just sitting across from him was intimidating, but he actually seemed to want her to answer questions that she couldn't.

"What are your future plans?" he asked her.

She sighed. "I've been trying to find someone to help me figure that out."

He smiled. "Then perhaps I am that someone. Tell me what your problems are."

It all came pouring out. She told him about her uncertainty about a career, her desire to go to college but the resistance she had met from her guidance counselor, even her bewilderment about how she kept ending up in the spotlight.

He listened patiently, asking the occasional question. When she was finished, she looked at him helplessly, wondering if he actually could help her.

"I have my own theories about your future, which I shall share with you at a later time," he admitted.

She was stunned. She still couldn't believe that the owner of The Zone was trying to help her with her insignificant problems.

"I believe you'll figure out in time what you want to do with your life. I think that you will find that you are meant to spend more of that life in the spotlight than you ever guessed. There is an old saying, 'Some are born great. Others have greatness thrust upon them.' I have a feeling you are marked for greatness. Don't let anyone ever tell you otherwise. Apply for whichever colleges you wish, though I would strongly recommend Florida Coast as one of your selections. Draw up a list of all the things you've accomplished in the last several months to show to your guidance counselor. Also, send me the names and the addresses of the colleges of your choice, and I will personally send a letter of recommendation on your behalf."

"I don't know what to say," Candace stammered.

" 'Thank you' should do in this situation," he said.

"Thank you."

"You're welcome. Now, is there anything I can do to help you with Sugar Shock?" he asked.

Candace smiled. "You could help me acquire some prizes for the costume contest."

He glanced at his watch. "I have some time right now."

"Perfect."

They left the Comfort Zone and headed for the shops of the Home Stretch.

They walked into the first store, and stunned silence greeted their arrival. Candace smiled to herself. The two celebrities of The Zone were appearing together. They went through every store in the Home Stretch, choosing prizes for the costume contest. In the end they had more than Candace believed she could possibly hand out, and he helped her carry them back to the Comfort Zone.

"Thank you again," she said.

"Thank you for taking this event to heart," he said. "You're really breathing fresh life into it, and I appreciate that."

"I hope the kids do too," she said.

18

The night of Kurt's Halloween party arrived. Candace admired herself in her mirror and then picked up the phone and called Tamara. "I love you even more now. The makeup goes perfectly with the outfit."

"Told you," Tamara said. "I gotta run. My parents and I just took our seats, and the play's about to start. Have fun and call me in the morning."

"I will," Candace promised. She hung up the phone and did a slow turn. It was odd. Kurt was the only one she knew at The Zone who hadn't said anything about her recent adventures. She wasn't sure why, but she was trying not to let it get to her.

"I love what you did with my hair," she called out to her mother.

Her mom came into the room. "Well it seemed to me that a Greek goddess should have intricately braided hair around her laurel leaves."

"You were right. It's perfect. Thank you."

"You're welcome. We haven't had much of a chance to talk," her mom said, sitting down on her bed. "Are you okay?"

"Yeah. I'm still a bit jumpy, but I'm doing okay," Candace said.

"Your father and I are very proud of you. We're still upset that you didn't tell us what was going on, but we are very, very proud."

"Thanks," Candace said, giving her mom a quick hug.

"You know, I've been watching you the last several months. You're becoming quite a woman."

Candace blushed. That was high praise coming from her mom who didn't usually wax so sentimental.

"I think you're really beginning to find your way."

"It's starting to feel like that, but I still think I have a long way to go," Candace admitted.

"But you'll get there, I'm sure of that. You're much more mature than I was at your age."

"Really?"

"Really. Have fun tonight. Just remember to call if you need us."

"I will," Candace promised.

The doorbell rang. "That's Kurt," Candace said, suddenly feeling breathless with excitement.

"Knock him dead, sweetie," her mom said.

"I will."

Downstairs she heard her dad open the door and greet Kurt. She paused and then left her room and walked down the stairs as regally as she could. She had half expected to see Kurt dressed like a historical character. Instead she was surprised to see that he had opted for dressing like a mime.

"You look great," he said appreciatively when she reached the door.

"Thanks. So, can you actually mime?" she asked.

He pantomimed trying to get out of a box.

"Okay, enough. I see that you can."

He smiled. "You know, a mime is a terrible thing to waste."

She groaned.

"Have fun," her dad told her before kissing her cheek.

"Thanks, Dad."

Once inside the car, she turned to Kurt. "So, you really like my costume?"

"Love it. Which goddess are you?" he asked.

She thought he must be teasing. "Which one do you think?"

He looked serious. "Hmmm ... are you Hera, the wife of Zeus?"

"No."

"Artemis?"

"No," she said, starting to feel irritated.

"Then who?"

"Aphrodite."

"Oh, of course, the goddess of love. I like it."

"You should. That was the first romantic dinner we shared ... at Aphrodite's."

"Sorry! I totally should have picked up on that. My bad."

"That's okay. You'll just have to make it up to me."

"I can certainly do that."

"So, who's going to be at the party?" she asked.

"Well, my roommates and I are throwing it, so a lot of the people are friends we have in common. But a few are just friends of one of them, and then you're the only person they don't know."

"Well, then, I'm honored," she said. "I haven't met your roommates before."

"They're great guys," Kurt said.

"So what are we going to do? Play games? Dance?"

"Probably hang out, socialize, talk a lot. There'll probably be music at some point, and where there's music there's usually dancing."

"You should have warned me so I could brush up on my conversation skills," she said.

"I think you speak the language of love perfectly."

And you're forgiven, she thought.

A few minutes later they arrived at Kurt's apartment. She walked inside and felt a bit of excitement. So, this was where Kurt lived. He introduced her to his roommates.

"Brian, Jim, this is my girlfriend, Candace."

"Pleased to meet you," Brian said.

Jim just nodded at her.

"It's good to meet both of you," Candace said.

Jim nodded again, and then the two moved off. *Guess I didn't have to worry too much about what we were going to talk about*, she thought.

More people came through the front door, and they moved out of the way. "Let me give you a quick tour," Kurt said.

"Okay."

"So, this is obviously the living room."

He headed down a hallway, and she followed. "This is the bathroom," he said, waving to it as they walked by. They passed a couple closed doors and at the end of the hall Kurt opened the third and stepped inside. "And this is my room," he said.

Candace stepped inside and couldn't help but feel a little self-conscious. There were a couple of movie posters up on the walls, a bed in the one corner, and a desk jammed into the opposite corner. The desk was piled high with textbooks, and a computer whirred loudly.

Before she could say anything, someone shouted Kurt's name. She followed him back out into the hallway and into the living room. He then spent five minutes introducing her to various people whose names and faces blurred together. Candace eventually found a seat on one of the sofas, and Kurt wandered off to greet some more people.

"Wanna drink?" one of Kurt's roommates, she thought it was Jim, asked her. He was holding out a cup that smelled strongly of alcohol.

Candace wrinkled her nose. "No, thank you."

"Not thirsty, or a prude?" he asked.

"Are you drunk?" she countered.

"I hope so."

"Hey, Jim, bring that drink over here," a girl who looked younger than Candace called.

Jim stood up and headed over toward her.

"What's wrong?" Kurt asked, reappearing. "You look like you just smelled a skunk or something."

"You didn't tell me you were going to be serving alcohol," Candace said.

Kurt shrugged. "I'm not serving it. My roommates are. They're both over twenty-one."

"Yeah, but not everyone who's drinking is," Candace pointed out.

Kurt shrugged again. "Neither of us is drinking, so what's the big deal?"

The big deal was she didn't like seeing people getting drunk. She had been to dinners and parties with her parents where people drank, but not like this. She saw one girl in the corner drunk out of her mind, making out with some guy who kept asking her what her name was. Her parents had let her taste the occasional drink when she was younger, and she'd tried just enough to know that she hated the taste. Even if that weren't the case, though, she wouldn't drink until she was twenty-one, and she certainly wouldn't drink to the point where she did things she wouldn't do otherwise.

She stood up and walked out onto the balcony, badly in need of some fresh air. Kurt followed her and stood next to her, gazing out across the parking lot for a minute. "Look, if you don't want to be here, we can go somewhere else."

"I wouldn't want to make you leave your party," she said.

He didn't answer that, and she felt disappointed. She wanted to go. She wanted him to go too. Not because he felt like he had to go with her, but because he didn't like the behavior of the people there anymore than she did. She couldn't even begin to imagine what another half hour of drinking would reduce some of them to.

Kurt's other roommate staggered onto the balcony. "Dude, you're missing all the fun. Come on."

"Just a minute," Kurt said, looking irritated.

"Go ahead," Candace said. "I'm tired and a bit cranky. Sorry. I think I'm just going to head home."

"I'll drive you," Kurt said.

She found it significant that he didn't protest. She wasn't sure if that was because he respected her wish to go or if it was because he would be relieved if she did. "I've already been a pain. I don't want you to miss your party," she said. "I can call Tam and get a ride."

"Are you sure?"

"Yeah."

"Okay. I'll see you later?"

"You bet."

He bent down and gave her a swift kiss before heading back inside. Candace lingered on the balcony for a moment before going back into the apartment and making her way to the front door. She slipped outside and walked down to the parking lot, flipping open her phone.

It was only then that she remembered that Tamara was at a play with her parents.

"Great." She thought of calling her parents. They'd come get her in a heartbeat, but she wasn't in the mood to tell them why she was leaving the party early. Another thought occurred to her.

"Hello?" Josh answered on the second ring.

"Hey, it's Candace."

"Hey! What's up? How's Kurt's party?"

"Not exactly my speed. Listen, I know this is a huge favor to ask, but is there any way you could pick me up?"

"Of course. Are you okay?" he asked.

"Yeah. I'm in the parking lot."

"I'll be there in fifteen minutes."

"Thanks," she said.

He made it there in twelve. "Thank you so much," Candace said as she got into his car.

"Don't worry about it. You look great, by the way. Let me guess. Aphrodite, the goddess of love?"

"Very good," Candace said, checking out his costume. "I have to say, though, your Superman costume is impressive."

"What costume?" he asked.

"True. You certainly rescued me."

"So, where to?"

"I don't know," she said, leaning her head back and closing her eyes.

"Have you eaten yet?"

"No."

"Neither have I. Let's get something."

"Works for me."

"So, what happened?"

"I don't want to talk about it," she said.

"That's cool."

There was silence for a moment, and then she couldn't help herself. "There was alcohol at the party."

"Oh."

She knew from the tone of his voice that he understood and that she wouldn't have to tell him anything else. Somehow that made it easier to open up.

"There were people drinking who were under twenty-one. Worse, some of them were pretty drunk."

"It's sad that so many people think they have to drink to have fun. In reality the best parties are the ones where everyone stays sober," Josh said.

"That's how I feel. I mean, it's not fun to watch some girl my age, plastered out of her mind, getting felt up by a guy she doesn't even know."

"That's not cool," Josh said. "Did Kurt tell the guy to back off?"

"No."

"Oh."

"At least not while I was there," Candace said. "Maybe he did after I left."

They pulled into the parking lot of a Denny's. Candace turned to look at Josh. "Aren't you afraid people will discover your secret identity?"

"No. I've managed to fool a lot of people for a long time. Besides, you're the only one who knows, and you're not going to tell."

"Nope. I'll never tell anyone that you're Clark Kent," she said jokingly.

He smiled at her in a way that let her know that he appreciated the joke, but that even more he appreciated the fact that she did know his one real secret and that she would never tell anyone.

"Speaking of secrets, you still owe me one," he told her.

"I guess I do." She sighed. "The one secret I've got right now is that I sometimes worry that there's no real future with Kurt."

"I'm sorry," he said.

She shrugged. "Let's get some dinner."

A minute later she laughed when she caught their reflections in a mirror. "Aphrodite and Superman went into a Denny's," she said.

"And they said to the waitress . . ."

"I don't know, but there has to be a good punch line in there somewhere," Candace said.

"And yet, somehow I don't think that was it," Josh said.

They were quickly seated, and Candace was further amused to note that they were not the only patrons in costume. At least half the people in the restaurant were dressed up. "It's getting to be a regular freak show in here," she heard one of the waitresses joke to another.

After they had ordered, Candace asked Josh, "Do you think I was being too sensitive about the party?"

He shook his head. "I would have left too. I've never been accused of being overly sensitive, so go figure."

"I just hope I didn't embarrass Kurt by leaving so abruptly," she said.

"Hey, as I see it, he's the one that should be embarrassed for taking you some place that made you uncomfortable," Josh said. "It's his problem. Not yours."

Across the room someone dropped a tray, and dishes hit the floor with a crash. Candace jumped several inches off her seat and yelped. Josh looked at her, startled.

"You okay?"

"Yeah, sorry. My nerves are just a bit fried."

He nodded. "Totally understandable with everything that's happened. Something happens to people during Scare. There's a lot of stimuli, people lunging out of the dark, loud noises, all of that. It can make some people a bit jumpy and they don't have half the excuses you have."

"Just call me some people."

"That's one thing I would never call you. You are unique, special. I still can't believe how you chased down Will like that. That was truly awesome. Crazy, but awesome."

Candace blushed. "It was no big."

"Yeah right. I know you're terrified of mazes. You chased him through one—that's big in my book. If it hadn't been for you, Scare might have been ruined."

"Thanks," Candace said.

"No problem. You need to learn to take more pride in your accomplishments."

"I guess I just feel like they're not really mine, you know? It's like the Party Zone. That name was a no-brainer. I have a hard time believing I was the first one to come up with it, and yet everyone makes a big deal. Now this. I was in the right place at the right time to help, that's all."

"But you did help. That's the huge part. A lot of people wouldn't. A lot of people don't care enough to try and make a difference. You do."

Candace smiled. "Okay, so I need a few lessons in tooting my own horn. I'll work on it."

"Thank you. You know, I heard they're thinking of turning your latest adventure into another maze next year," Josh said with a sly grin.

Candace threw a piece of ice from her water glass at him.

"Joking, joking," Josh said, hands raised in front of him. "Call off your missiles."

19

Halloween, or Shock Day, as Candace had started calling it, arrived. She woke in the morning. The skies were light without a cloud in them. It looked like it was going to be a beautiful day. The rain the weatherman had predicted had decided to cut her some slack.

She dressed and got to The Zone as quickly as she could. Martha was already waiting for her in the Comfort Zone with a dozen other referees to whom she was giving assignments. It would be the base of operations for the entire event and as such was going to see heavy traffic from key referees.

"I'm coordinating the parade," Josh said with a grin.

"I'm helping with the prizes for the costume contest," Roger told her.

"I'm keeping the candy stations stocked," Megan added.

"I'm taking tickets at the gate," Becca said, a sad look in her eyes.

"I promised Gib you wouldn't even be here," Candace blurted out before she could stop herself.

Gib, it turned out, was behind her. "The Muffin Mansion crew are here, all of us. We figure it's the least we could do after you saved the park."

"Thank you," Candace said, humbled by the show of support.

Martha handled the briefing before sending everyone out to do their assigned jobs. "Let's move, people. One hour to Shock!"

"And you are going to be running the costume contest," Martha said. "We'll be using the stage at the Party Zone."

"But I need to help run things," Candace protested.

"You're the woman of the hour, and we need you where everyone can see you."

"You mean, I'm not going to be directing things from up here?" Candace asked.

"That's right. I'm kicking you out of your comfort zone."

From the look on Martha's face, Candace knew she had intended the pun. She sighed and headed out into the park.

Sugar Shock officially started at eleven, and the costume contest was scheduled to begin at twelve thirty. Candace ran around checking that everyone had what they needed before the park opened.

Finally the moment of truth arrived. The gates opened and Becca took the first ticket.

Candace roamed the park, overseeing everything that was going on and trying to find Sue. At last she spotted her friend in between a little boy dressed like a Jedi and a little girl dressed like a princess. They had to be Sue's siblings.

Candace ran up to them, and before Sue could say anything, she dropped down on one knee. "You wouldn't be Gus and Mary, would you?" she asked the two children, both of whom were staring at her wide-eyed.

They both nodded. "How did you know?" Gus challenged.

"I'm a friend of your sister's," Candace admitted.

"This is Candace," Sue told them.

"Cotton Candy!" Mary said. "We've heard all about you!"

"Sorry," Sue said, looking embarrassed.

"Don't worry about it," Candace said. To Mary she said, "I used to be Cotton Candy over the summer, but now I'm Candy Corn."

"Why is that?" Gus asked.

"Because I'm so corny," Candace joked. "Either that, or it's because I have special treats for kids like you." From behind her back she produced two giant candy-corn-shaped lollipops. "Don't let the other kids see. It will make them jealous," she said.

Gus and Mary took the lollipops and stuffed them quickly into their bags, both quivering with excitement.

"So cool," Mary cooed.

Candace stood up.

"Thank you," Sue said. "That was really sweet."

"Don't mention it. You're the only person I know who was bringing kids. I had to spoil somebody. One of the perks of helping organize this thing."

"You've done a great job," Sue said.

"It's even better than last year," Gus said solemnly.

"Why, thank you," Candace told him.

"We've already got twice as much candy," Mary said.

"Then everything is going according to plan," Candace said.

In truth, the whole thing was going better than she could have hoped. She was especially happy that she had found Sue so she could give away the special treats she'd found for Gus and Mary.

"Well, we should go get the rest of the candy," Sue said.

"Thank you, Candy Corn," Gus and Mary chorused together.

"You're welcome," she said.

"I'll see you tonight," Sue said.

"You bet."

Candace watched as Gus and Mary started running, dragging Sue with them. Everywhere she looked she saw kids doing the same thing to parents, grandparents, and older siblings. Everyone was laughing and having a good time.

Candace glanced at her watch. She had fifteen minutes before the costume contest was set to start. She walked slowly toward the Party Zone, enjoying seeing all the kids filling their bags with more candy than they could eat in a month.

Roger joined her in the Party Zone, a huge bag of prizes at the ready. They had broken the contestants up by age and category, including: funniest, prettiest, scariest, most original, and best replica. Stuffed animals, T-shirts, stickers, DVDs, and more came out of the sack. There were enough prizes for each child that entered the competition. Four jumbo stuffed animals were awarded to the 'best of show' in each age group. Candace was having the time of her life. It was way better than just handing out bite-size pieces of candy. At three o'clock Sugar Shock came to a close. The janitorial staff swept in to clean up the candy wrappers and spilled sodas. The leftover candy was distributed at the End Zone to the children as they left, but not before Gib had escorted Becca to her car.

Within an hour the entire thing was cleaned up. Candace walked through The Zone, amazed at how hard and how fast everyone had worked. Sugar Shock had been a success, and she was grateful. With only two and a half hours left before she would have to get her cart ready for Scare, she climbed back to the Comfort Zone.

Martha waved at her, and Candace staggered into one of the side rooms to lie down on a cot. "All I need is two hours," she muttered to herself as she flipped onto her side.

She had just drifted to sleep when she heard someone walk into the room. "Hey, Candace."

She opened her eyes and saw Kurt. He sat down on one of the other cots.

"Hey. How did you get in here?"

"Lots of people coming in and out, and one of them didn't know I wasn't supposed to be here."

"Oh."

"I hear Sugar Shock went well."

"Very well," she said, unsuccessfully stifling a yawn.

"Congratulations."

"Thanks."

"I just wanted to apologize."

"For what?" she asked. He had to be talking about the party.

"For not talking to you about the other night when you caught those guys."

"Oh." Candace struggled to sit up a little.

"I play a hero every day in this park, but when my girlfriend was in real danger, I was nowhere around."

"Kurt, that's not your fault."

"I keep telling myself that, but it doesn't make me feel any better. To tell the truth, I'm not sure if I could have been all heroic and saved you even if I had known."

"Don't beat yourself up about it," she urged.

"A little late for that."

"Well, I forgive you, if that helps. But I never expected you to come riding in on a white horse and rescue me."

"I would have liked to."

"That means a lot," she said. "Is that why you were acting weird at the party?"

"I don't know, I guess," he said with a shrug.

Well, that was better than nothing.

Kurt just sat there, brooding silently. Finally Candace had to break the silence. She needed to get some rest, and she wasn't going to be able to as long as he was sitting there staring.

"Is there anything else?"

He shook his head and stood up. "No. Happy Scare."

"Happy Scare to you too," she said with a smile.

He walked out, and after a moment she lay back down. She wished she could tell what he had been thinking, but he'd tell her when he was ready.

She had just drifted away again when someone else called her name.

She opened her eyes and saw that it was now Roger who was sitting on the cot across from her. "I need to ask you a question," he said.

"At least you're supposed to be here," she said.

"What?"

"Nothing. What was it you wanted?"

"A question answered."

"What am I, the guru of The Zone?" she joked.

He didn't answer. "I want to ask out Becca. Do you think she would say yes?"

She looked at him for a moment. It seemed like an unlikely pairing, but obviously he had been thinking about her quite a lot. "Go for it!"

"You think?"

"Yeah. I mean, what's the worst that can happen? She says no and you guys have the same relationship you do now."

"You're right," he said, jumping to his feet. "I'm going to ask her tonight."

"Good for you."

Roger rushed out and her head hit the pillow hard.

Candace got a total of maybe fifteen minutes of sleep. After Roger, at least a dozen other people had come in to say something or ask her something. As she staggered, bleary eyed, toward the carts, she wondered if she would have been better off just staying up.

"Candace!"

She turned and saw Sue jogging up.

"I don't have any more advice left in me," Candace said.

"Okay. I wasn't looking for any."

"Oh good. What's up?"

"We have to meet at the Holiday Zone tonight before taking our places. Didn't you see the flyers?

In truth she hadn't. She followed Sue over to the Holiday Zone where everyone had gathered. A minute later several referees appeared, carrying a throne on which John Hanson sat. He was dressed as a scarecrow and wore a crown on top of his head.

"Who's he supposed to be?" Candace asked.

"The Scare King," someone whispered.

"Another year, another Scare!" he shouted.

The crowd cheered and whistled.

"In a few minutes Halloween night will be upon us and with it the howling monsters, the crazy witches, and the ravenous wolves. Of course, I'm talking about the players!"

Everyone cheered and laughed.

"Tonight, enjoy yourselves, have fun, and most of all Scare the living daylights out of them!"

The crowd roared and the Scare King stepped down off his throne and walked amongst his people.

"You have to admire his style," Candace said to Sue.

"You really do," she agreed. "Thank you, by the way, for the special treats for Gus and Mary. They loved them."

"I was just glad I could do it," Candace said.

The crowd began to disperse, and she headed for her cart. Like the Scare King had said, the ravenous wolves were about to descend, and she knew they'd be wanting their candy corn.

It turned out the cart led her right back to the Holiday Zone. Candace took up position close to the exit of Candy Craze. Somehow, she never seemed to leave it, she thought with a smile.

"Candace?"

She turned and saw Lisa standing there, dressed as Candy. The other girl looked wildly uncomfortable. "Thank you."

"For what?"

"I know you could've had this part back if you wanted it," she said.

Candace didn't like Lisa. Still, the other girl's distress made her feel sorry for her. "Don't worry about it. Just be the best Candy you can be," she said with a smile.

"I will!" Lisa promised before turning and running toward the entrance to the maze. She stopped short and turned back around. "Oh, and I've been practicing something."

"What?"

Lisa threw back her head and gave a bloodcurdling scream that could rival Candace's own.

"You go, girl," Candace shouted when Lisa had finished.

Within minutes the players swarmed into the park in twice the numbers of the previous nights. It seemed like every last one of them wanted candy corn. For three hours Candace filled one order after another.

A referee ran by screaming, followed by another.

"The pirates are marauding!" someone shrieked as they rushed by her cart.

"Isn't that what pirates do?" Candace called out.

"You don't understand," the girl yelled back, pointing the way she had come. "They're marauding this way!"

And then Candace heard them.

She turned and saw the horde sweeping toward her, players scattering before them. Suddenly they were at her cart. Candace screamed as they began to grab bags of candy corn and toss them to the crowd waiting for the maze.

"What are you doing?" she yelled, trying to wrestle the bags away from them.

"We're liberating this cart!" Gib shouted.

"But you can't! Whose going to pay for these!"

"All you need to see is this," Gib said, pulling a piece of parchment from his vest. "Letters of Mark from the Scare King. This cart and all its candy corn is ours!"

"What?"

Gib leaned close. "These letters give us the right to do as we see fit according to the contract between us and the Scare

King. And if you're worried about the pay, recheck your till. The Scare King anticipates all."

Candace moved to the side and watched in amazement as they redistributed all the candy corn. Then she saw something terrifying. Becca had a bag of candy corn in her hands.

"No!" Candace yelled, reaching for her.

It was too late. Becca downed half the candy corn in one swallow. "Oh dear," Candace breathed.

And suddenly it was as though there were a dozen Beccas. She was everywhere at once, moving at lightning speed and shrieking. She brandished her sword and led a charge against a group of referees who had clustered nearby.

Candace saw Becca trip and twist her ankle. A moment later Becca was up and had climbed onto Gib's back. "Hop!" Becca screamed, waving her sword. Gib led the rest of the pirates as they chased after the other referees.

Candace just stood stunned. "What just happened?" she asked in bewilderment. Her cart whirred to life, and she followed it back to the cart station where it shut back down and refused to budge.

Candace sat down and laughed hysterically. Martha finally came by. Candace told her what had happened. Martha's radio came to life, and Candace could hear security officers across the park talking to each other. It sounded like they were planning some sort of assault against the Pirate Queen.

Martha handed Candace a bag. Candace looked inside and saw her Candy costume. "What's this for?" she asked.

"You know what they say. Two Candys are better than one."

Candace hugged Martha and then ran to change. On her way to Candy Craze, she saw the pirates. Becca was still on Gib's back shouting "Hop!" They had pinned down the security forces who had been fools to go in after them.

She ducked into the Candy Craze and found Lisa. Lisa took the first three runs through the maze while Candace took the last two. Suddenly the wait time was cut in half. None of the players seemed to notice or care that it was a different girl.

"Good to have you back," Ray said.

"Better to have you back," Candace joked as she struggled against him.

Players streamed through the maze, screaming at the top of their lungs and stampeding at every turn. Candace gave them the best show that she could. After all, that was what Scare was all about.

20

The first rays of the sun swept the horizon and shone their light on the park. The darkness fled before it, and the monsters crept out of their mazes and into the light. Candace could hear several giving thanks that the night was over. She had never been so tired in her entire life, and it felt good.

They all moved together toward the center of the park where they gathered in small clusters, exchanging stories, comparing bruises.

Candace looked at her friends. Most of them looked as tired as she felt. Roger had blood smeared on his chin, and Candace was pretty sure it was real. Sue's mummy bandages were unraveling, and a four-foot train fluttered behind her like she was some kind of demented mummy bride. Josh was completely white despite the fact that his makeup had worn off hours before. Becca was asleep perched on Gib's back. Gib himself was swaying on his feet as though he was going to fall over at any moment.

"I survived the Inquisition!" a ragged-looking ref said.

Pete grabbed him by the shoulders and shook him. "Pull yourself together, man. That's at Knott's Berry Farm!"

Candace wanted to smile, but she was too tired. Of all of them only Josh was still smiling. Candace noticed, though, that when the others weren't looking he winced in pain and he was not putting much weight on his right foot.

John Hanson appeared in the middle of the crowd, a bull-horn in hand. "I want to thank you all for a great night! Thanks to your hard work this has been the most successful Scare of all time!"

A weak cheer went up from those assembled.

"I appreciate the way you all pulled through. I've never seen a finer example of teamwork either on field or off."

The cheers were a little louder.

"And to thank you all, it's time to head on over to the Party Zone for a catered breakfast!"

The cheers were deafening.

The owner of the park led the way, his followers trailing behind. Candace smiled as she wondered if the Israelites had looked like such a ragged group as they followed Moses out of Egypt and toward the Promised Land.

Josh fell into step next to Candace, and she could definitely ascertain that he was limping. "Are you okay?" she asked.

He smiled. "Nothing an ice pack and a day of sleep couldn't fix," he said.

"I hear that."

"What'd you think of your first Scare?" he asked.

She pondered briefly how to answer that. It had been terrible and wonderful. It had stretched the limits of what she thought she could endure and tested her courage and fortitude. It had brought her to the depths and sent her to the heights. Excitement and fear, anger and peace, joy and sorrow had all come in their time. *To everything there is a season, and a time for every purpose under heaven. And this is my fall.*

To Josh she summed it up the only way she could. "It was life changing."

He nodded as though he understood the meaning more fully than even she did. "You're not the first to say that," he said.

"And I'm sure I won't be the last," she finished.

"True."

They made it to the Party Zone to find heaping platters of steaming pancakes, scrambled eggs, bacon, fruit, cereal, coffee, juice, and a minature replica of the Muffin Mansion built entirely out of muffins.

Exhausted as she was, there was one thing that Candace wanted more than sleep … and that was food. She filled her plate until she was afraid things were going to start sliding off the top and then sat at a table with old friends and new.

Across from her, Reggie lowered her hood, and Candace was surprised to find that Reggie was a girl roughly the same age as she was. Next to her, Ray also removed his hood, and Candace saw a kindly old man that looked a lot more like Santa Claus than a psycho killer.

She just started laughing. It was the magic that was Halloween at The Zone. Nobody was truly what they appeared to be. Yet young and old, high school students and grandparents—they could all join together for a few special nights to scare the daylights out of their fellow men.

Josh lifted his glass of juice into the air. "A toast to Scare and to Halloween. Praise God they only come once a year!"

"Hear! Hear!"

Candace raised her own glass of juice in salute. She could definitely drink to that. As awesome as it had been, as good as she felt, she was pretty sure she'd need about a year to recover.

When breakfast was over, Candace hobbled toward the Locker Room to collect her things. Sue walked beside her. Around them other referees moved just as slowly.

"The lists are out for the people who've made it through the first round of the scholarship competition!" someone in the crowd yelled.

"What?" Candace asked.

"You know, the competition where you submit a ride drawing and the winner gets a full ride to Florida Coast," Sue said.

"If I'd had any talent for that kind of thing, I would have totally entered."

"I think Josh mentioned something about that over the summer," Candace said.

"Come on, let's go see the list," Sue said.

A few minutes later Sue and Candace were standing in front of the list.

"Martin from janitorial, good for him!" Sue said. "I saw his drawing and it looked pretty cool. I don't know a couple of these people. Oh, look, Rick from the front gate. Wow!"

Candace could only see one name on the list. She blinked several times. It was impossible. There was no way she could be reading it right. And then Sue saw the name too.

"Candace, that's you!" she shrieked. "You didn't tell me you entered."

"I didn't," Candace said, dazed. "There must be some sort of mistake."

"No mistake," a familiar voice said behind her. "I entered you in the contest."

Candace turned around and stared at Josh. "How on earth did you manage that?" she asked.

He shrugged. "You gave me your Balloon Races sketch. The rest of the information I needed wasn't too hard to get."

She wasn't sure how to feel. Part of her felt violated. There was another part, though, that was excited. Someone liked her sketch. She had a chance of winning a full scholarship because of it.

"Well, are you going to hit me or hug me?" he asked finally.

"I'm still trying to decide," she said.

"Fair enough."

"What happens now?" she asked.

"Now everyone who works for The Zone has the opportunity to submit recommendations for people on the list. The top candidates after that are interviewed and the final selection made."

"That sketch was nothing," she said.

"I disagree. And clearly, so do the judges," he said. "To have made it this far means that several Game Masters looked over your design, liked it, and thought it was viable."

"What happens if it wins?"

"You get a full scholarship, and they build your ride."

For just a moment she imagined what it would be like to be on a ride she had created. That tipped the scales and made her decision easy. She hugged Josh. "Thank you."

"You're welcome," he said.

She felt tears sting her eyes. Just a few weeks ago she had been told she had no ambition, and she herself had admitted to having no focus, no path. Somehow, though, Josh had a different view of her. He had seen promise where she herself hadn't been able to. Suddenly she wanted very much to win.

"What's wrong?" Josh asked.

She pulled away. Both he and Sue looked worried. She dashed the tears away. "It's just that Tamara was right. For someone who says she doesn't like the spotlight, I seem to find it an awful lot."

Sue smiled and Josh laughed. Candace hugged Sue and then Josh again. It was good to have friends.

🍁

Candace walked into her guidance counselor's office on Monday afternoon with a piece of paper clutched in her hand. She sat down across from him and looked him in the eye.

"Good morning, Candace. How can I help you?" he asked.

"I don't think our last meeting went very well. You didn't have a complete picture of what I bring to the table as far as college applications," she said.

"Really?" he asked, his eyebrows raised in surprise.

"Yes," she said, handing him the piece of paper.

He took it and began to read it over. "You're involved with your youth group and are going to be leading a new Bible study starting this month. You're involved with the drama class.

You worked the Scare event, and you helped organize and run the Sugar Shock for The Zone this year."

He paused and looked up at her. "Really?"

"Yes."

"I took my kids to that, and they went crazy."

"In a good way?" she asked cautiously.

"Yeah, they loved it. It was much better than last year."

"Thank you."

He looked back down at the paper. "It says you're also a semifinalist for The Zone Game Master scholarship."

"Yes. I just found that out yesterday," Candace said.

"Wow. I think you're right. You do have a lot more to bring to the table than I initially thought. I'm impressed."

"Thank you."

"So, refresh my memory. The Game Master scholarship is for Florida Coast, correct?"

She nodded. "That's correct."

"So, have you always been interested in theme park design?" he asked.

"To be honest, I never thought about it until a good friend suggested that I give it some thought. Then it turned out my ride sketch, which was really more of a doodle, got me to the semifinals of the scholarship competition. I think at this point I'd be crazy not to at least consider it as an option."

"Certainly. I mean, if you have a talent for that, it would be a shame to waste it."

"Mr. Anderson, I believe you are a Zone fan," Candace said.

"Season ticket holder," he admitted.

She smiled and leaned back in her chair. "Let's discuss my other college options," she said, smiling.

An hour later Candace left Mr. Anderson's office feeling positive about the future. School was already out. She called Tamara to pick her up and then listened to a message from Josh. She called him back.

"Hey, how'd your meeting with the guidance counselor go?" he asked.

"Really well," she said. "He seems a lot more positive about my future, and so do I."

"That's awesome! I want to hear all about it. I also wanted to help you think about some of your short-term goals."

"Uh-huh. Why do I sense that there's more work coming my way?" she asked suspiciously.

"Come on, I think you'd be great as one of Santa's elves."

"Doesn't he bring his own with him from the North Pole?" she asked.

"Nah, they're too busy making toys. We provide him with temporary elf help while he's visiting."

"I see," Candace said. "And just what would I have to do?"

"It's a no-brainer," he teased.

"Oh, no."

"That's right."

"Don't tell me."

"Yup."

"Oh come on."

"You guessed it. You'd be passing out candy canes."

Of course she would.

A Sweet Seasons Novel

the winter of candy canes

debbie viguié

**Read chapter 1 of The *Winter of Candy Canes*,
Book 3 in Sweet Seasons.**

1

Candace Thompson was once again eye-to-eye with Lloyd
Peterson, hiring manager for The Zone theme park. This time,
though, she felt far more confident. She had already spent her
summer working as a cotton candy vendor, and she had worked
one of the mazes for the annual Halloween event. She had even
saved the park from saboteurs.

Now she was back, and this time she was interviewing for
a job working the Christmas events at the park. Surely after
everything she had done for the Scare event, she had nothing
to worry about. She tucked a strand of red hair back behind her
ear as she gazed intently at the man across from her.

"So you want to work Holly Daze?" he asked.

She nodded. Christmas at The Zone was a big deal, and the
park began its official celebrations the day after Thanksgiving.

"You keep hiring on for short bursts of time and then leaving. Do you have some sort of problem committing to things?"
he asked, staring hard at her.

She was stunned, but answered, "I don't have any problem with commitment. I signed on to do specific things, and the jobs ended. That's not my fault. I didn't quit."

"So, you plan on making a habit of this?" he demanded. "Are you going to show up here again in a couple of months expecting me to give you some kind of job for spring break?"

"No, I—"

"I know your type," he said, standing up abruptly. "You're just a party girl. No commitments … no cares … just grab some quick cash and get out. You think you can handle Holly Daze? Well, you can't! You're weak and a quitter. You're going to bail on me as soon as your school vacation starts, and then what? Well, let me tell you, missy. You aren't wanted here. So just pack your bags and get out!"

By the end of his tirade, he was shouting, eyes bulging behind his glasses and tie swinging wildly as he shook his finger under her nose. Candace recoiled, sure that he had finally flipped out. *I'm going to end up as a headline: Girl Murdered by Stressed-Out Recruiter*, she thought wildly. *Well, I'm not going down without a fight!* She jumped to her feet and put some distance between her and the wildly wagging finger.

"You need to calm down!" she said, projecting her voice like her drama teacher had taught her. Her voice seemed to boom in the tiny office. "Pull yourself together. You're a representative of this theme park, and there is no call to insult me. Further- more, I'm not a quitter. I'll work for the entire Christmas season. Then the next time I come in here, I'll expect you to treat me with some respect. Do you even realize what I've done for this park so far? Seriously. Take a chill pill."

She stopped speaking when she realized that he had gone completely quiet. She held her breath, wondering when the next explosion was going to come. Instead, he sat down abruptly and waved her back to her chair.

"Very good. You passed the test," he said, picking up a pen.

"What test?" she asked, edging her way back into the chair.

"The ultimate test. You're going to be one of Santa's elves."

"Doesn't Santa, you know, have his own elves?" she asked, still not sure that he was completely in charge of his senses.

"Of course Santa has his own elves. However, when he's here at The Zone we supply him with courtesy elves so that they can continue making toys at the North Pole," Mr. Peterson told her.

"So, I'm going to be a courtesy elf?" she asked.

He nodded and handed her a single sheet of paper. "Sign this."

She took it. "What? Just one thing to sign?" She had expected another huge stack of forms that would leave her hand cramped for hours afterward.

He nodded curtly. "You're now in our system as a regular seasonal employee. All of your other paperwork transfers."

"Regular seasonal" sounded like some kind of contradiction to her, but she was still not entirely convinced his outburst had been a test. She scanned it, signed her name, and then handed it back to him.

"Good. Report to wardrobe on Saturday for your costume fitting," he said.

"Okay, thank you," she said, standing up and backing toward the door.

"Welcome back, Candy," he said, smiling faintly.

"Thanks," she said, before bolting out the door.

As soon as she was outside the building, she whipped out her cell phone and called her friend Josh, a fellow employee of The Zone.

"Well?" he asked when he picked up.

"I think Mr. Peterson has seriously lost it," she said. "He totally flipped out on me."

Josh laughed. "Let me guess. You're going to be an elf."

"So he was serious? That was some whacked-out test?"

"Yeah. Elves are considered a class-one stress position, and it can get pretty intense."

"How hard can it be to be an elf?" she asked.

She was rewarded by a burst of laughter on the other end.

"Josh, what is it you're not telling me?"

He just kept laughing.

"Okay, seriously. You were the one who convinced me to work Holly Daze. I think it's only fair you tell me whatever it is I need to know."

"Sorry!" he gasped. She wasn't sure if he was apologizing or refusing to tell her.

A girl bounced around the corner and slammed into Candace.

"Josh, I'll call you later," she said, hanging up.

"Sorry," Becca apologized.

Becca was one of Candace's other friends from the park, one who had some sort of bizarre allergy to sugar that made her uncontrollably hyper. Candace looked suspiciously at Becca. Her cheeks were flushed, her eyes were glistening, and she was hopping from one foot to the other.

"You didn't have sugar, did you?" Candace asked, fear ripping through her.

"No! Promise," Becca said.

"Then what gives?"

"Roger made me laugh really hard," Becca explained.

Roger had a crush on Becca and had wanted to ask her out since Halloween. It hadn't happened yet.

"Oh," was all Candace could think to say.

"So, are you working Holly Daze?" Becca asked.

"Yeah. I'm going to be an elf."

Suddenly, Becca went completely still, and the smile left her face. "I'm sorry," she said.

"Why?" Candace asked.

Becca just shook her head. "I've gotta get back to the Muffin Mansion. I'll catch you later."

She hurried off, and Candace watched her go. *Okay, now I know there's something people aren't telling me.*

She debated about following Becca and forcing her to spill, but instead she headed for the parking lot where her best friend Tamara was waiting. She walked through the Exploration Zone, one of the several themed areas in the park.

The Zone theme park was created and owned by John Hanson, a former professional quarterback who believed in healthy competition at work and play. His theme park had several areas, or zones, where people could compete with each other and themselves at just about anything. Almost everyone who worked at The Zone was called a referee. The exceptions were the costumed characters called mascots. Most of them, including Candace's boyfriend, Kurt, were to be found in the History Zone. People visiting the park were called players, and the areas of the park they could reach were called on field. Only refs could go off field.

Candace cut through an off field area to get to the referee parking lot. She waved at a few other people she recognized from her time spent working there. Finally, she slid into her friend's waiting car.

"So are you going to be the Christmas queen?" Tamara asked.

"What am I, Lucy VanPelt? There's no Christmas queen in Charlie Brown's Christmas play, and there's no Christmas queen in The Zone," Candace said.

Tamara fake pouted. "Are you sure? I think I'd make a beautiful Christmas queen."

Candace laughed. Tamara was gorgeous, rich, and fun. Her whole family practically redefined the word *wealthy*, and, with her dark hair and olive skin, Tamara was usually the prettiest girl in any room. She didn't let it go to her head, though. Anybody who knew Tamara would vote for her as Christmas queen.

"Although I think you would, they're only hiring elves."

"You're going to be an elf?" Tamara smirked.

"Hey, it beats being a food cart vendor," Candace said.

"But you're so good at it. Cotton candy, candy corn ... you can sell it all."

"Thanks, I think. So, what are we doing tonight? Kurt's going to swing by at six to pick us up." Just mentioning her boyfriend's name was enough to make Candace smile. She closed her eyes for just a minute and pictured him as she had first seen him—wearing a Lone Ranger costume. With his charm and piercing blue eyes, she had fallen for him right away.

"You told him my house, right?" Tamara said, interrupting her thoughts.

"Yeah. So, who's this guy you're taking?"

Tamara sighed. "Mark."

"Uh-huh. And?"

"Remember my cousin Tina?"

"Yeah."

"Well, she broke up with him over the summer, and he's been all shattered since then. He won't date other girls; he just mopes over her."

"Attractive," Candace said sarcastically.

"Tell me about it. Well, Tina asked me if I could help him get his confidence back and get over her or something."

"A pity date? Are you kidding me? You want Kurt and I to double date with you on a pity date?"

"You don't think I'm about to go by myself, do you? No way. That's the best-friend creed. When you're happy, I'm happy. When I'm miserable, you have to be too."

"Great," Candace said, rolling her eyes. "So, where are we going?"

"That's the problem. I was thinking dinner, but then we'd have to talk, and frankly, I don't want to hear him go on about Tina. Then I thought we could see a movie."

"You wouldn't have to talk to him," Candace confirmed.

"Yeah, but what if—"

"He tries to grab a hand or put his arm around you."

"Exactly, and I don't think me giving him a black eye was what Tina had in mind."

"I guess that also rules out any kind of concert possibilities?" Candace asked wistfully.

"Yup. Sorry."

"So, what did you come up with?"

"I was thinking … theme park?"

"No way. Kurt doesn't like to spend his downtime there."

"I thought he took you to that romantic dinner there over the summer."

"It was the nicest restaurant he knew, and he got an employee discount."

"Charming," Tamara said.

"Plus, ever since we got trapped in there overnight, he's been even more adamant about avoiding it when he's off work."

"I can't believe you two get to be the stuff of urban legend, and you don't even appreciate it."

Candace sighed. It was true that she and Kurt had spent one of the most miserable nights of their relationship trapped inside the theme park. Urban legend, though, had since transformed the story so that they were supposedly chased through the park by a psycho killer. It was still embarrassing to have people point at her and say that she was the one. Around Halloween she had given up trying to correct people. They were going to believe what they wanted.

"Earth to Candace. Helloooo?"

"Sorry. So, what does that leave us with? Shopping?"

"No need to torture both our dates," Tamara said.

"Then what?"

"I don't—miniature golf!" Tamara suddenly shrieked, so loudly that Candace jumped and slammed her head into the roof of the car.

"Tam! Don't scare me like that."

"Sorry. Miniature golf. What do you think? Built-in talking points, lots of movement, and zero grabby potential."

"I like it. I'll have to borrow one of your jackets though."

"At least you'll have an actual excuse this time," Tamara teased.

A few minutes later they were at Tamara's house and upstairs raiding her wardrobe. As Tamara considered and discarded a fifth outfit, Candace threw up her hands.

"Maybe if you'd tell me what you're looking for, I could help."

"I'm looking for something, you know, nunlike."

Candace stared at her friend for a moment before she burst out laughing. She fell to the floor, clutching her stomach as tears streamed down her face. Tamara crossed her arms and tapped her foot, and Candace just laughed harder.

"I don't know why you think that's so funny. You know I don't go past kissing."

"Tam, nuns can't even do that. And if you're looking for something that will completely hide your body, then you're going to have to go to the mall instead of the closet. You don't own anything that doesn't say 'look at me.' I'm sorry, but it's true."

"Really? Maybe we should go to your house. Think I could find what I'm looking for in your closet?"

"Not since I started dating and mom made me throw out all my old camp T-shirts," Candace said with a grin.

"Then hello, you've got no call to laugh."

Candace stood up, stomach still aching from laughing so hard. "Tam, I'm not criticizing. I'm just telling you, you're not going to find what you're looking for."

Tam reached into the closet. "Oh, yeah, what about this?" she asked, producing jeans and a black turtleneck.

"If you're going for the secret agent look, it's a good choice."

Tamara threw the jeans at her, and Candace ducked.

"I could wear some black pants with this. Would that be too funereal?

"For a pity date? Go for it."

Candace opted to borrow Tamara's discarded jeans instead of wearing the skirt she had brought with her. They turned out to be slightly tighter on her than they were on Tam, and she had to admit when she paired them with her red scoop-neck top that she looked really good.

When Kurt arrived a few minutes later, he whistled when he saw her.

"Keep the jeans," Tamara whispered to her. "Obviously, they work for you."

Kurt then looked at Tamara and frowned slightly. "Did you just come from a funeral?"

"No, but thank you for thinking so," Tamara said with a smirk.

"I don't—"

Candace put her finger over his lips. "Don't ask," she advised him.

He smiled and kissed her finger, which made her giggle.

The doorbell rang again, and Candace turned, eager to see the infamous Mark.

Tamara opened the door, and Candace sucked in her breath. Mark was gorgeous. He had auburn hair, piercing green eyes, and model-perfect features. He was almost as tall as Kurt, and he was stunning in khaki Dockers and a green Polo shirt.

"Hi," he said, smiling.

Tamara glanced at her and rolled her eyes.

"Hi, Mark."

Kurt drove, and Candace was quick to slide into the front seat with him, leaving Tamara and Mark to the back. She shook her head. Mark was not her idea of a pity date in any sense of the word. Maybe Tamara would come around if she actually talked to him.

They made it to the miniature golf course and were soon on the green. Candace got a hole in one on the first time up to putt, and Kurt gave her a huge reward kiss.

When they moved on to the next hole, Tamara whispered in her ear, "Thanks a lot. This is supposed to be a no grabby zone. Now Mark will be getting ideas."

"Tam, you really need to relax a little."

They made it through the course in record time, and Kurt gave Candace another kiss for winning by one stroke. After turning in their clubs, the guys headed inside to order pizza while Candace and Tamara went to the restroom.

"This date is the worst," Tamara groaned once they were alone.

"What's wrong with you? He's gorgeous."

"Really? I guess I just can't see past the Tina mope."

"What mope? He hasn't even mentioned her, and he's done nothing but smile all night. You should totally take him to Winter Formal."

"No way. This is a one-date-only kind of thing. I'm not taking him to Winter Formal."

"Fine. Suit yourself. I'm just telling you that if it weren't for Kurt, I'd be taking him to Winter Formal."

Tamara laughed.

"As if. There's no way you'd ask a guy out."

"I don't know. You might be surprised."

"It's a moot point anyway. I'll find someone to take."

"You could always take Josh," Candace suggested.

"You're not setting me up with Josh, so just forget it."

"Fine."

"Find out for me, though, if Santa needs a Mrs. Claus," Tamara said.

"You're going to find some way to be the Christmas queen, aren't you?" Candace asked.

"Even if I have to marry old Saint Nick."

They both laughed.

Carter House Girls Series from Melody Carlson

Mix six teenage girls and one '60s fashion icon (retired, of course) in an old Victorian-era boarding home. Add boys and dating, a little high school angst, and throw in a Kate Spade bag or two ... and you've got the Carter House Girls, Melody Carlson's new chick lit series for young adults!

Mixed Bags

Book One

Softcover • ISBN: 978-0-310-71488-0

Stealing Bradford

Book Two

Softcover • ISBN: 978-0-310-71489-7

Homecoming Queen

Book Three

Softcover • ISBN: 978-0-310-71490-3

Viva Vermont!

Book Four

Softcover • ISBN: 978-0-310-71491-0

Books 5–8 coming soon!

Pick up a copy today at your favorite bookstore!

Visit www.zondervan.com/teen

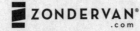

ZONDERVAN®
.com

Forbidden Doors

A Four-Volume Series from Bestselling Author Bill Myers!

Some doors are better left unopened.

Join teenager Rebecca "Becka" Williams, her brother Scott, and her friend Ryan Riordan as they head for mind-bending clashes between the forces of darkness and the kingdom of God.

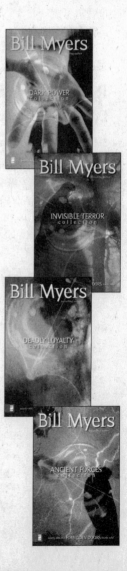

Dark Power Collection
Volume One

Softcover • ISBN: 978-0-310-71534-4

Contains books 1–3: *The Society,*
The Deceived, and *The Spell*

Invisible Terror Collection
Volume Two

Softcover • ISBN: 978-0-310-71535-1

Contains books 4–6: *The Haunting,*
The Guardian, and *The Encounter*

Deadly Loyalty Collection
Volume Three

Softcover • ISBN: 978-0-310-71536-8

Contains books 7–9: *The Curse,*
The Undead, and *The Scream*

Ancient Forces Collection
Volume Four

Softcover • ISBN: 978-0-310-71537-5

Contains books 10–12: *The Ancients,*
The Wiccan, and *The Cards*

Echoes from the Edge

A New Trilogy from Bestselling Author Bryan Davis!

This fast-paced adventure fantasy trilogy starts with murder and leads teenagers Nathan and Kelly out of their once-familiar world as they struggle to find answers to the tragedy. A mysterious mirror with phantom images, a camera that takes pictures of things they can't see, and a violin that unlocks unrecognizable voices ... each enigma takes the teens farther into an alternate universe where nothing is as it seems.

Beyond the Reflection's Edge
Book One

Softcover • ISBN: 978-0-310-71554-2

After sixteen-year-old Nathan Shepherd's parents are murdered during a corporate investigation, he teams up with a friend to solve the case. They discover mirrors that reflect events from the past and future, a camera that photographs people who aren't there, and a violin that echoes unseen voices.

Eternity's Edge
Book Two

Softcover • ISBN: 978-0-310-71555-9

Nathan Shepherd's parents are alive after all! With the imminent collapse of the universe at hand, due to a state called interfinity, Nathan sets out to find them. With Kelly at his side, he must balance his efforts between searching for his parents and saving the world. Will Nathan be reunited with his parents?

Book 3 coming soon!

Pick up a copy today at your favorite bookstore!

Visit www.zondervan.com/teen

Share Your Thoughts

With the Author: Your comments will be forwarded to
the author when you send them to *zauthor@zondervan.com*.

With Zondervan: Submit your review of this book
by writing to *zreview@zondervan.com*.

Free Online Resources at
www.zondervan.com/hello

 Zondervan AuthorTracker: Be notified whenever your favorite authors publish new books, go on tour, or post an update about what's happening in their lives.

 Daily Bible Verses and Devotions: Enrich your life with daily Bible verses or devotions that help you start every morning focused on God.

 Free Email Publications: Sign up for newsletters on fiction, Christian living, church ministry, parenting, and more.

 Zondervan Bible Search: Find and compare Bible passages in a variety of translations at www.zondervanbiblesearch.com.

 Other Benefits: Register yourself to receive online benefits like coupons and special offers, or to participate in research.